Guardian Academy, Book Two

ENTANGLED

JESSICA SORENSEN

Entangled
Jessica Sorensen
All rights reserved.
Copyright © 2016 by Jessica Sorensen
ISBN-13: 978-1533117250

This is a work of fiction. Any resemblance of characters to actual persons, living or dead, is purely coincidental. The author holds exclusive rights to this work. Unauthorized duplication is prohibited.

No part of this book can be reproduced in any form or by electronic or mechanical means including information storage and retrieval systems, without the permission in writing from the author. The only exception is by a reviewer who may quote short excerpts in a review.

Any trademarks, service marks, product names or names featured are assumed to be the property of their respective owners, and are used only for reference. There is no implied endorsement if we use one of these terms.

For information: *jessicasorensen.com*

Cover Designed by:
Najla Qamber Designs

Interior Design & Formatting by:
Christine Borgford, Perfectly Publishable

ENTANGLED

CHAPTER ONE

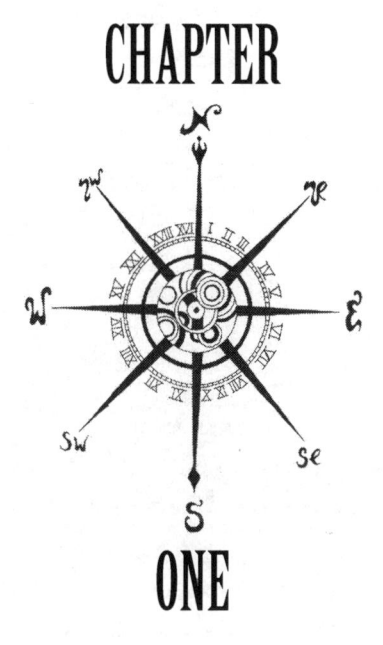

MY KNEES KNOCK TOGETHER AS I press my back against my locked bedroom door. Worry slams through me as I stress over the meaning of the mark painted on the hallway floor. Someone from the Electi is probably here at the academy. And they know I know about them.

Crap. Crap. Crappity crap. I'm so dead.

"Grandpa, can you hear me?" I call out to the darkness.

The lights are off in my overly small dorm room, and every shadow makes me feel jumpy. But I'm not about to turn the light on and declare where I am.

"I don't know what to do. You keep telling me I can't trust people, but I think I need to tell someone about the mark on the floor."

Silence clings to the air. I'm alone unless whoever painted

the mark is lurking around. *Waiting to kill me.*

No one has flat out told me that the serpent shaped in a backward three represents the Electi group, but I'm ninety-nine percent sure it does. From what Jax told me, the Electi run experimental paranormal facilities and have been causing the Guardian's investigation rate to skyrocket through the roof. He also told me they'd kill me if I found out about them. According to my grandpa Luca, though, they don't want me dead. They're watching me, wanting me as an experiment subject. I don't understand why. I'm nothing extraordinary. Why not just kill me, instead?

That's the million-dollar question.

After I jiggle the doorknob to make sure the door is locked, I cross the room and scoop up my phone from my unmade bed. I don't know who to call, but I have to tell someone or Vivianne Monarelle—Head of Interrogation and the woman in charge here at Guardian Academy—will probably blame the paint-on-the-floor incident on me. She's already convinced my grandpa stole the Dagger of Conspectu before he died and that he gave it to me. Technically, that's true. But I know there has to be a good reason he took the dagger, and until I find out why, no one's getting ahold of it.

But do I really know him like I thought I did?

I recall the cracked crystal ball Jax and I found near a murder crime scene a couple of days ago, which turned out to be my grandpa's traveling crystal ball. I don't know how it got there since he has been dead for over a week now, but I was worried enough that I talked Jax into holding off for a bit before we turn it in as evidence. I don't believe my grandpa had anything to do with the murder. At least, I don't want to believe he did.

Maybe I really didn't know him as well as I thought.

No. I won't go there, not until I have all the facts.

I take a few measured breaths then punch in Jax's contact

number. He's probably still pissed off at me for using the truth serum on him, but right now, he's the only person at the academy I can trust.

"Hello," he answers after four rings. A loud pop song booms in the background and mixes with the noises of people laughing and shouting.

"Um, hey . . . This is Alana."

"I know," he says flatly. "Your number's programmed into my phone."

"Oh." Yep, he's definitely still pissed off.

I don't really blame him. The serum forced him to divulge the truth to me about the Electi, and he accidentally confessed his attraction to me, too. That part, I didn't want to hear. Okay, that might be a bit of a lie. Jax is annoyingly intense sometimes, but I'll admit to being stupidly flattered he thinks I'm beautiful.

"Did you need something?" he asks impatiently.

I clear my throat. "I need your help with something."

"I'm kind of busy right now. Can it wait?"

A girl giggles. "Come on, Jax. Let's go dance."

I consider hanging up because clearly he's "busy," but I need his help.

I force the sweetest tone I can muster. "Look, I hate to break up whatever you've got going on, but this can't wait." I take a breath, preparing for how angry he's going to be. "I was just about to fall asleep when I heard someone whisper how I should've left it alone, and now there's a serpent shaped in a backward three painted on the floor just outside of my room."

"Where are you right now?" Panic flares through his tone.

"In my room."

"Is the door locked?"

"Yes."

"Do you have a weapon on you?" he asks, the music and laughter fading.

"I have a baseball bat." I bend over and scoop the bat off the floor.

"Good. Stay in the room until I get there," he says in a rush. "Is your roommate with you?"

I glance at the empty, made bed across from me. "No. I've barely even seen her since I got here, and the one time we crossed paths, she slammed the door in my face."

"Well, she's breaking rules by not being in her dorm room this late." He speaks loudly over the roar of a car engine. "I'm going to report her."

"It's probably good she's not here." I peek out the window where the moon graces the star-kissed sky then at the silhouettes of the trees surrounding the academy.

My room is on the first floor. If someone wants to get in, all they'd have to do is break the window. And while I can kick ass when I need to, I'm not sure how my badass kickboxing skills would measure against these Electi since I know very little about them and their talents. I don't know if they're strong, have magical skills, or what.

I inch closer to the window and scan the darkness outside, searching for someone or something lurking out there. "The mark on the floor . . . It's the Electi's mark, isn't it?"

"Yeah." He pauses, and then I hear a loud bang. "Goddammit, Alana! Why the hell couldn't you just let this go? I was trying to protect you, and you just had to keep pushing it. Now they know you know. I'm surprised they haven't killed you already."

"I'm sorry, but I needed to know who they are. It was important." Tears burn in my eyes, but I suck them back.

"Why was it so important? And how did you even find out about them in the first place? Hardly anyone knows they exist. And you want to know why? Because they're all dead!"

"You're not dead yet, so I guess they don't kill everyone."

While I know I'm in some deep shit, if I ever want to clear

my grandpa's name, I need to get to the bottom of what was going on before he died and why he was talking with the Electi. Finding out who the Electi are was the first step in solving the mystery surrounding his death.

"Do you even realize how much trouble you're in?" Jax bites back. "They're probably either dragging out your death to mess with you, or they're going to haul your ass to an experimental facility the second they get ahold of you."

"I don't know why they'd take me to a facility. I'm just a Guardian."

"They've taken Guardian's before. They've taken Keepers and Foreseers and witches and zombies. They'll basically take anyone with a drop of supernatural blood in them."

"Oh." I frown but force the poutiness out of me. "Look, I get that I'm in some serious crap, but I needed to find out who they are, and you are the only person I knew who seemed to know about them."

Silence fills the line.

"Why did you need to know so badly?" he asks, sounding a tiny bit calmer.

I press my lips together and take a breath to steady my voice. "Because I did."

Another lengthy pause.

"Do you know something about something?" His tone conveys a cautious edge.

"I know a lot of somethings about somethings."

What does he know about this? I haven't told anyone about my grandpa and the things he told me while he dream-walked into my dream or the stuff he still tells me now by whispering in my thoughts. The only person who knew he was involved in something before he died is my grandma, but she doesn't know it was the Electi, just that my grandpa spoke to a man with a serpent mark.

"Wait. Do you know something about something?"

"Maybe." He hesitates. "A case might have just come in involving a person who may have allegedly been involved with the Electi. Although I'm not completely buying it, I think there's more to his story than what's in the file."

I chew on my thumbnail. "Do I know this person?"

"You do, but what I want to know is how you found out this person was associating with the Electi before they died, because I haven't told anyone that detail about the case yet." He gives another long pause. "Did this person tell you something before they died?"

I'm terrified to utter the words aloud, but I think it might be time. "We are talking about my grandpa, right?"

He exhales in relief. "I was beginning to worry we were going to tiptoe around that all night."

"Well, I didn't want to out his secret if you didn't know about it. Everyone already thinks he was a terrible person."

"I don't think that. I think he just got mixed up in some stuff and got way in over his head."

I rest my elbow on the windowsill and stare out into the night. "So, you don't know why he was talking to the Electi before he died?"

"I don't *yet*, but I'm going to get to the bottom of it," he promises. "I think you might need to tell me everything you know, though."

"Okay." I hesitate, unsure where to start. "I think—"

A high-pitched, shrill noise bursts through the line.

I cringe, my eardrums ringing. "Holy crap. That sounded like a dying alien." I plug my nose and puff out my cheeks, pressurizing my ears. "Did you drive through a tunnel or something? Where are you, anyway?"

"I had to do something tonight," he says. Another shrill screech blasts through the line again, and he curses. "Look, I'm about an hour away from the academy." His tone turns stone cold. "I'll call you when I get closer. I need to focus on driving. Just make sure to keep ahold of that bat."

The line goes dead.

I move the phone away from my ear and frown at the "call ended" flashing across the screen. "Man, werewolves are so moody sometimes."

Setting my phone down on the dresser, I grasp the baseball bat in my hands and hurry to the other window to get a better view of the front of the school. Night blankets the grounds, and every shadow or movement sends a chill down my spine. What if someone's out there, watching me from the forest?

"Why the hell would they be watching me, though?" I mutter to myself. "What do they want from me?"

They're only watching you right now because you're not ready yet, my grandpa whispers through my thoughts.

"Dude, grandpa, I love you and everything, but this whole ominous, cryptic, tiptoeing-around-the-subject thing is starting to get on my nerves. Can't you just tell me everything so I can solve your case and take these Electi bastards down?"

I can't . . . I wish I could . . . but I'm . . . too . . . His voice drifts away like the wind.

I let out an exhausted sigh. Too many questions, not enough answers. Maybe Jax can tell me more when he gets here. Am I ready to tell Jax everything I know and how I know it? I'll probably sound one step away from being in a straightjacket.

Before I can start psycho-analyzing myself, headlights spotlight through the darkness as a car turns into the driveway of the academy. I press my face to the glass and squint to get a better look.

The car parks in the driveway in front of the entrance doors of the school, and then Vivianne Monarelle climbs out. She's not alone, either. A beautiful woman with long, lily white hair; pale skin; and flawless features gracefully slides out of the passenger seat. At first glance, she looks human, but under her glamour, her eyes that appear blue are hollow and sunken in, leafy vines curve around her boney arms, and her ghostly white hair moves like snakes.

What. The. Hell? Why is Vivianne Monarelle having a midnight rendezvous with the Empress of the Water Fey? I mean, I know the water fey can wander away from the lake now, but no one's supposed to know they're free except for a handful of Keepers and the Foreseers.

Hmmm . . . Just what is Vivianne up to?

I lean to the right to get a better look as the two of them meet at the front of the car and hurry into the forest, casting worried glances over their shoulders. I reach for my phone to call my dad and tell him what I just saw, but a knock on my door interrupts me. I tense, gripping the bat as the doorknob wiggles. Someone bangs on the door again, and I reel back to the window, debating if I should make a run for it.

I'm reaching for the latch when a dark blur zooms across the lawn and vanishes into the forest. A howl echoes through the night, one I'm pretty sure belongs to a werewolf. But there's no full moon, so it doesn't make any sense.

Another knock comes from the door, this time hard enough to send a framed photo off the wall. The doorknob twists, and my breath catches in my throat as the metal lock breaks apart. Whoever's out there is freakishly strong and desperately wants to get in.

I raise the bat, ready to fight for my life, as the door swings opens.

CHAPTER TWO

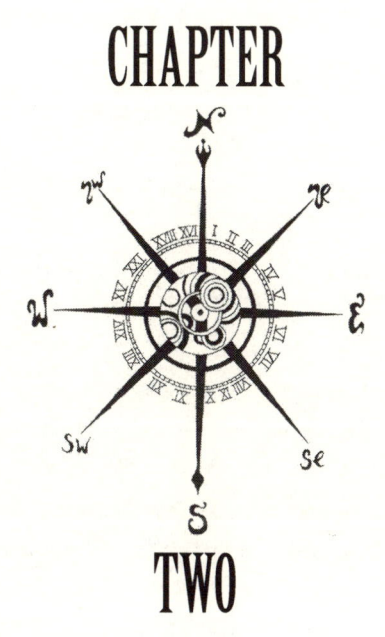

I STRIDE FORWARD, PREPARING TO swing the bat at the hugely tall, sturdy figure looming in the doorway.

"Get the hell away from me," I growl, "or I'll beat the shit out of you."

"I'm s-sorry." He hurriedly puts his hands to his sides. "I-I didn't mean to. Dash said—"

"Don't blame this on me," Dash says, waltzing into my room and pulling the other guy in with him. "I told you to pick the lock, not snap the door in half."

The guy grumbles, "Yeah, I guess you're right."

Dash lets go of the guy, kicks the door shut, and strolls past me like he owns the place. My nostrils are instantly overwhelmed by the delicious scent of his cologne mixed with sugar. Why does the guy always smell like yummy cookies?

"You're being watched," Dash mutters, peering out the window. The moonlight trickles in from outside and highlights his concerned expression.

"I know that." I lower the bat, my gaze bouncing back and forth between the guy by my door and Dash. "Okay, so I don't want to sound like a bitch, but why are you here? And why the hell did you break my door?"

"I didn't break your door. Thad did." Dash hitches his thumb over his shoulder, pointing at the large guy standing a few feet away from me.

"Sorry," Thad murmurs, scuffing the tip of his clunky boot against the floor. "It was an accident. I was trying to pick the lock but gripped the knob too tightly."

Okay, Mr. Holy Human Super Strength. He seems like he feels bad about it, though, so I offer him a smile.

"No worries. It's just a door." I turn back to Dash and point the end of the bat at him. "You didn't answer my other question."

"I thought that was pretty obvious," he says. "We're here to rescue you."

"Who said I needed rescuing?" Or did he see the mark painted on the floor outside and just assume?

He glances at me with his brow curved upward. "You really don't know?"

I shake my head then pause. "Jax called you, didn't he?"

"He did, but he didn't mention why I needed to run to your room at"—he glances at his watch—"twelve-thirty at night. I'm guessing it has something to do with that mark painted on the floor outside your room."

A thought strikes me out of a blue. Dash was in the room when Jax told me about the Electi. Dash knows about the Electi. That means he's in danger, too. But why didn't Jax just tell Dash the reason he needed to come to my room? Could it be because Thad's here?

"Jax mentioned I needed to stay in your room until he gets here and that I'm supposed to beat the shit out of anyone who comes in." Dash opens his arms to the side, his lips twitching with amusement. "You'll be more safe if I hold you. We can lie in the bed, too, if you want. Just a warning, though, my hands have minds of their own. I take no responsibility for where they try to wander."

"I think I'm okay just hanging onto the bat." *Don't smile. It'll only encourage him.* "And FYI, I'm not helpless. I know how to beat the shit out of someone when I need to." I nod my chin in the direction of Thad. "I was about two seconds away from kicking his ass."

"Thad's a little clumsy. I bet you could kick his ass." Dash offers Thad a somewhat apologetic look before his gaze lands back on me. "He's part ogre, though, so it's not his fault."

My head whips in Thad's direction, and I instinctively shuffle back. From what I was taught, ogres are supposed to be large creatures with pointy ears and fangs who like to snack on humans. While Thad is on the tall and broad side, I don't see any fangs, pointy ears, or gleaming hunger in his eyes.

I loosen my grip on the bat. "You don't look like an ogre."

"That's because he's only half-ogre." Dash moves up behind me and positions an elbow on my shoulder. "If you look close enough, you can see some of the resemblance. He won't hurt you, though."

Thad stares down at his feet with his shoulders hunched.

Feeling bad for the way I first reacted, I step toward him with the bat lowered at my side and extend my hand. "I'm Alana Avery. Sorry for acting all weird. I was just a little surprised. I've never met an ogre before."

"It's okay." He takes my hand and gives it a hard shake, nearly jolting me off my feet. "I get that a lot. Most people won't come within a hundred feet of me."

"People can be such assholes," I say as he releases my hand from his death grip.

A tiny drop of a smile touches his lips. "Sorry about your door. Sometimes, I don't know my own strength."

"That's okay." I flex my fingers, which are cramped from how tightly he gripped my hand. "I'm sure it can be fixed."

Thad notes the unmade bed. "Will your roommate be mad when she finds out?"

I prop the bat against the metal footboard of my bed. "My roommate doesn't come into our room that often, so I doubt she'll find out if I get it fixed quickly enough."

Thad rakes his fingers through his cropped brown hair, frowning at the broken door knob busted to pieces on the floor. "I'll fix it first thing tomorrow morning so you won't get in trouble."

I smile warmly. "Thanks. That'd be awesome."

"You should stand in front of the door, at least until Jax gets here, and make sure no one gets in," Dash tells Thad, removing his elbow from my shoulder.

Nodding, Thad slumps his weight against the door, securing it shut with his body. "No one'll get through. I promise."

Dash starts wandering around the limited space of my bedroom, looking at the scuffed floor, the bland walls, and the tile ceiling. When he passes the lamp on my nightstand, he tugs on the cord, and soft light filters through the room.

The first thing I notice is Dash and Thad are both dressed in black jeans and zipped up hoodies. Mud cakes the bottom of their black boots, fingerless leather gloves cover their hands, and Dash has a couple of leaves and twigs stuck in his dark brown hair.

I find their appearance odd. Just where the heck were they before they came here? In the forest? That's weird since I just saw Vivianne, the Empress, and maybe a werewolf duck into the trees.

Dash stuffs his hands into the pockets of his hood and leans forward to examine a photo of my grandpa and me taped to the wall above the nightstand. "That's where you get your violet eyes from, huh?"

I nod, stepping up beside him. "My mother's eyes are the same color, too."

He glances at me from the corner of his eye. "When I first met you, I thought maybe it was because you were a pixie, but then I realized you were too nice to be a pixie."

"I'm not that nice," I argue. "I can be mean when I need to."

He smirks at me. "It's cute you think that."

I glower at him with my hands on my hips, but it's more of a joking move than anything. "You wouldn't be saying that if you really knew me. I was mean to your brother when I first met him."

"Ha, I wish I could've seen that." He grins. "He's not used to people throwing his own personality in his face. I bet he got so pissed."

"He was. He even threatened to kill me," I tell him. "I don't really think he would've, though."

"I don't know. It was a full moon that night," Dash muses, thrumming his finger against his lips. "He can get awful cranky during a full moon."

Huh? How does Dash know I met Jax on a full moon?

Dash quickly clears his throat, looking away from me. "So, why does my brother think someone might be trying to kill you now?"

"Did he use the word *kill*?" I watch him roam around the room as I question the abrupt subject change. He's hiding something from me, something about that night in the club when I met Jax.

"No, but he sounded really uptight. More than he normally does." Dash opens the top drawer of my dresser where I keep all my underwear and peers inside.

"Whoa, whoa, whoa." I jump forward and slam the drawer shut. "What's up with the snooping?"

"Just seeing when you'd stop me." His smirk makes another grand appearance. "Didn't peg you for a lace girl."

I narrow my eyes at him with my arms folded. "No more snooping through my stuff."

He grins innocently at me as he crosses his arms and leans against the wall. "What? It's not like I knew they were in there."

I fight back a smile. He isn't funny. He isn't cute. Okay, he kind of is. Whatever.

"Did Jax say when he'd get here?"

"He said a little over an hour," he replies. "I don't know where he was when he called. He hardly ever leaves the academy this late unless he's called on a case. But he said he wasn't on one."

I sink down on the bed and tuck my hands under my legs. "I think he might have been at a bar or club or something. When I first called him, there was some loud music playing in the background, and it sounded like a ton of people were around."

Dash's brows spring up. "Jax? At a club? *Really?*"

"That's what it sounded like." I tuck a strand of my long, brown hair behind my ear. "A girl said something to him while we were on the phone. I think he might've been on a date or something."

Dash exchanges an amused look with Thad then seals his lips together, repressing a laugh.

I look back and forth between the two of them. "What's so funny?"

"Jax being on a date," Dash says. "He's been on, like, three, and all of them ended in a disaster because he's socially incompetent, way too uptight, and scares everyone off."

This bit of information surprises me. Jax did act kind of douchebaggy when I first met him, and he can still get intense, but he has a sweet, kind side—well, on rare occasions.

Dash searches my eyes. For what, I have no idea. All I really know about Dash is that he likes to joke around, smells like cookies, and is bound to Vivianne. I'm not sure how he's bound to her or why he smells that way. He's definitely not just a Guardian, though.

I open my mouth, figuring now is as good a time as any to ask, but before I can get the words out, Dash's gaze zips to the window.

"What on earth?" He tugs on the lamp cord, smothering the room in darkness, then peers out the window.

I slant forward to see what he's looking at and spot Vivianne and the empress dashing out of the forest. A light mist snakes from the trees and dances around their ankles as they hightail it across the grass and toward the car parked in the driveway. The mist could be as simple as fog, but I have the eeriest feeling it's linked to something paranormal.

"I saw them pull up to the academy about half an hour ago," I whisper to Dash. "And then they hurried into the trees. I saw a weird blurry thing go in there too, and then I heard a werewolf howl."

"Really?" He flicks a side glance at me. "That's weird."

"Yeah, I know," I whisper.

"How did the empress get out of the lake?" Dash whispers, inching closer to me.

I shrug, acting clueless. "I have no idea."

Dash's mismatched teal and silver eyes glimmer in the pale moonlight as he lowers his voice. "Do you know what I'm really curious about?"

I tense, fearing he can read through my lie. "What?"

He sneaks a glance from left to right then leans even closer. "Why are we whispering?"

I roll my eyes but smile. "It was instinctual, okay? Besides, you never know who could be listening."

His amusement dissolves as he returns his attention to the window. "Yeah, you're right."

Silence fills the room, and I reach for my phone to call my dad and tell him I saw the empress. The second I pick up my phone, though, Dash snatches it away from me.

"I'm under strict orders not to let you use your phone."

"Why not?" I lunge for the phone, but he tucks his arm behind his back. Letting out an exasperated breath, I plop my behind back down onto the bed. "So not cool, dude."

"Hey, I'm not the one who gave the orders." He slips my phone into the back pocket of his jeans. "All I was told was to come here and keep an eye on you, to bring Thad, and to keep you from using your phone."

My brows dip. "Why'd Jax say you need to bring Thad?"

"For extra muscle, I guess." He shrugs. "Jax can be kind of evasive sometimes."

"Yeah, I'm starting to notice that." My mood nosedives straight into the floor as a thought occurs to me. If Jax told Dash to bring extra muscle, then I'm guessing the Electi are strong.

"Just what is she up to?" Dash mutters with his nose pressed against the glass. "Yeah, I can see you, you little wench. I'm going to figure this out and destroy you."

"You don't like Vivianne, either?" I ask, leaning forward to get a view out of the window.

"Does anyone like Vivianne?" he mutters with his eyes fixed on the driveway.

I hug my knees to my chest. "I don't, but I thought maybe it was just me."

He shakes his head. "It's definitely not you. A lot of people would love to get her kicked out of the academy."

Restless, I push to my feet to stand beside him and look out the window. "Maybe we should report her for talking to the empress."

"Report it to who?" He squints at Vivianne and the empress who hop back into the car. "Vivianne's the Head of Interrogation; she's the one we're supposed to report these kinds of incidents to."

"I'm not talking about reporting it to the Guardians," I explain. "I think we should tell the Keepers. They might be able to look into it and find out more about what's going on."

Dash places his ear against the glass. "Just give me a second." He closes his eyes, concentrating.

"What are you do—"

He places a finger to my lip. "Shhh . . . I'm listening."

He can hear what they're saying all the way from here? Holy amazinginess, I'm impressed.

"I know. I'm super impressive." The corners of his lips pull into a lopsided smile, his eyes remaining shut. "And that's just one of my many, many talents." He removes his finger from my lips and presses his palm to the glass. "Wait a minute, I think I hear them . . . Yep . . . Oh, my word. I can't believe this."

"What is it?" I bite my nails in anticipation.

His eyelids open, and he dips his lips beside my ear. "They're exchanging cookie recipes."

I snort a laugh and playfully shove him away. "They are not. You're such a liar."

"I know." He sighs heavily. "I can't hear a damn word they're saying."

I glance from him to the car outside. "They're too far away?"

"No, it's not that." He paces the room. "It's way too quiet out there. I didn't even hear a cricket chirping."

Thad straightens but keeps his fingers enfolded around the

doorknob. "You think that's because of . . . ?"

Dash nods, cupping the back of his neck. "But why would she block me?"

"Maybe she wasn't trying to block you," Thad offers. "There's a lot of people in this school who could easily eavesdrop on conversations."

"What do you mean by *blocked*?" I move away from the window as headlights light up the strip of land in front of the school. "Like a witch's blocking spell? Is Vivianne a witch?"

"No." Dash stops pacing and looks at me. "But she might've gotten a witch to do it for her. Why, though? I mean, I know I don't like people listening in on my conversations, but I don't go around getting blocking spells put on me, either."

"Most people don't," I point out. "My aunt's a witch, and I've never had her put one on me. She did put one on my mom and dad for a while, but only when they were working on a secret project."

Dash taps his bottom lip. "I think I have an idea." When I open my mouth to ask what the idea is, he places his finger against my lips again. "Nope. Not going to tell you. That way, if I get caught and you get questioned, you can't be held accountable. The last thing we need is Vivianne having another reason to give you more detention."

I crinkle my nose. After spending the day locked in Vivianne's classroom, doing stacks of assignments, and then spending the evening with the janitor scrubbing down toilets, the last thing I want is more detention.

"Yeah, you're right," I say. "But you have to promise to tell me what you find out."

"Sure," he says, avoiding eye contact.

Yeah, that doesn't seem too promising. But why doesn't he want to tell me? And why does it feel like he knows more about this than he's letting on?

CHAPTER THREE

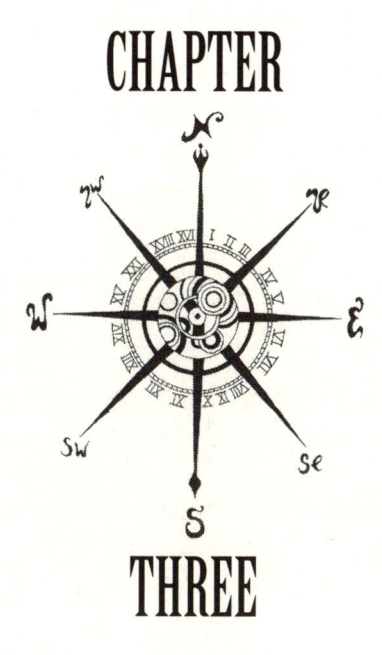

AFTER VIVIANNE AND THE EMPRESS drive away, Dash announces we need to do something fun instead of sitting around and worrying. Then he suggests playing spin the bottle or seven minutes in heaven. That's when I take things over and pull out a deck of cards.

"Aren't you just a party pooper?" Dash teases, sitting down on the floor beside me. He crisscrosses his legs and rests back on his hands. "I liked my suggestions better."

"You don't have to play cards if you don't want to," I tell him, shuffling the deck. "And you could always play your games with Thad."

Thad starts to sit down but freezes. "Wait. What?"

"She wants to see us kiss." Dash puckers his lips. "What do you think? Are you in or out?"

Thad rolls his eyes. "Definitely out." He sinks down beside me, the floor trembling beneath his weight.

Dash slips off his gloves and rolls up his sleeves. "I've never played cards before."

My eyes enlarge. "What the heck, dude? *Seriously?*"

He nods. "My mom and dad weren't really big on letting us play games."

I tap the side of the deck against the floor, aligning the cards. "Then what did you do for fun?"

He shrugs, unzipping his hoodie. "Train for becoming a Guardian. They were lucky we got marked with the Guardian mark, or all that training would've gone to waste." Sarcasm drips from his tone. "We were so far ahead of our peers when we came here that Jax skipped a lot of the beginner training classes."

I start dealing the cards. "What about you?"

He rolls up the sleeves of his hoodie. "I took a different route."

I set the deck down on the floor. "And what route was that?"

"The screw up and disappoint your parents route," he says casually, as if he is making peace with it. "Every family has to have a screw up, right?"

"I'm the only child, so I wouldn't know." I collect my dealt cards from off the floor. "I kind of get where you're coming from, though. Even though my parents seemed happy I got the Guardian mark, I could tell they were disappointed I wasn't going to follow in the family's footsteps and become a Keeper."

He collects the cards I dealt him. "Is everyone in your family a Keeper?"

"Most of them." I organize my cards from lowest to highest. "My grandpa was a Foreseer, though. When I was younger, I thought it'd be cool to be able to see the future. But when I got older, I realized what a huge responsibility it is. I mean, you know when everyone's going to die, when all the bad stuff is going to happen, and you can potentially have the power to alter all of it."

"Did your grandpa ever feel like that?" Dash frowns at the cards in his hands.

"Sometimes," I say. "But most of the time, he really loved being a Foreseer."

His frown deepens. "I wish I could love being a Guardian."

"You don't?" For some reason, that surprises me, maybe because Jax loves what he does so much.

He shrugs. "It's not that I hate it. I just don't love it. And unlike Jax, I'm not going to pretend to be the perfect son to please our father."

I set my cards on my lap. "Did you come here when you were fourteen like Jax?"

"Nope. I was sixteen. I got my mark when I was fourteen, but there were circumstances that . . . kept me at home." He brings his fist to his mouth and forcefully clears his throat. "So, what exactly am I supposed to be doing with these cards?"

I take the hint that he doesn't want to talk about this anymore and let the subject drop. "Here. I'll help you with the first few hands." I scoot over toward him and examine his cards. "So, you want to—"

The door suddenly jolts open and smacks against Thad's back. The three of us go rigid and jump to our feet with our hands clenched into fists.

"Let me in," Jax demands from the other side of the door.

"Oh. Sorry." Thad scoots out of the way.

The door swings open, and Jax barges into the room with fierce determination burning in his silver eyes. His gaze promptly sweeps the walls, the bed, the window, and then resides on the deck of cards. His brows knit.

"Are you guys playing poker?"

"What else were we supposed to do at two o'clock in the morning?" I ask, pushing to my feet.

"She's crazy, isn't she?" Dash says to Jax as he stretches his arms above his head. "I tried to talk her into spin the bottle, but she just wouldn't listen."

Jax glares at him. "You did *what?*"

Dash feigns innocence. "What? It's just a little kissing, and it's not like you haven't thought about doing it with her."

I shoot Dash a dirty look. "You seriously had to go there?"

Dash overdramatically covers his mouth with his hand. "Whoops. Was I not supposed to?"

Jax shakes his head at Dash. "Why is everything a joke to you?"

Dash shrugs. "I thought I was doing you two a favor. You know, clearing the tension in the air or whatever."

The two of them stare each other down. Their demeanor couldn't be more night and day: Jax intense and brooding and Dash . . . Well, honestly, he looks kind of bored.

Their personalities aren't the only things that are different. Even though they're twins and have similar facial features, they're fairly easy to tell apart. Jax's hair is light brown and styled in a fauxhawk, while Dash's is much darker and cut shorter. And, unlike Jax's silver eyes, only one of Dash's is silver, the other a vibrant shade of teal.

Dash finally raises his hands and steps back. "All right, you win this one."

Jax won't look me in the eye as he steps back and points at the door. "Thanks. You can go now."

He rolls his eyes then turns to me. "Have fun with Mr. Moody." He winks then heads for the doorway, stuffing his hand into his pocket, the same pocket he shoved my phone into earlier.

"Wait a second." I skitter in front of him and stick out my hand. "My phone, please."

"Phone?" His face contorts with confusion, but his eyes glitter with hilarity. "I don't remember this so-called phone. Are you sure you had one?"

"Dash, knock it off and give her the phone back," Jax warns. "Now."

"Relax. I'm just messing with her." He retrieves my phone from his pocket. "You need to chill out."

"You're chill enough for the both of us," Jax tells him with his arms crossed. "Now hand over the phone."

Dash glowers at Jax, but the look hastily fades as he moves to hand me my phone. But Jax snatches the phone from him before I can get to it.

"Hey," I protest, lunging for my phone, but he easily dodges out of the way. Frowning, I fold my arms and scowl at him. "What's up with all the phone stealing?"

Ignoring me, Jax shoves my phone into the back pocket of his jeans. "Thanks for keeping an eye on her," he tells Dash with a drop of sincerity.

"It's not like it was that big of a deal." He throws me another wink. "I mean, I did get to spend the night with a pretty girl."

I make a gagging face. "So cheesy."

He grins back before strolling out of the room with a swagger. Thad gives me a small, unsure wave before hurrying after him.

Once they're gone, Jax releases a stressed breath and pushes the door shut. "Goddammit, he can be such a pain in the ass."

I tug on the hem of my plaid shorts, feeling way under dressed in my pajamas compared to his black button-down shirt and dark denim jeans.

"He's not that bad. And it was nice of him to come keep an eye on me."

He cocks a brow at me. "Not that bad? Really? Did you hear anything he said?"

"What? He didn't do anything wrong. He was just joking around with the whole spin the bottle thing and the remark about the kissing . . . But yeah, anyway, I think it was pretty cool that he stopped whatever he was doing and came here to keep an eye on me."

"But the question is, what was he doing before he came here?" He rubs his jawline, staring out the window. "Did you notice the mud on his boots?"

"I did." I track his gaze to the forest. "Maybe he was doing something out there."

"That's what I'm afraid of," Jax mutters, worry creasing his brows.

"Why?" I ask. "Is there something weird in that forest?"

He nods. "As of yesterday, there is."

"What happened yesterday?"

"The morgue got moved to somewhere out there."

"Into the *forest*?"

"Yeah. It's not that strange. We move the location all the time." He looks away from the window, focusing on me. "Look, I know Dash is the fun, funny one, but he also does a lot of questionable stuff. You need to be careful what you do and say around him. I'm hoping you didn't tell him too much already, like about what was really going on tonight."

"I didn't. But I thought he already knew about the Electi? He was in the room when I . . ." I stop myself. Now is probably not the greatest time to bring that up.

He looks me dead in the eye. "When you stabbed me in the back and used truth serum on me."

Okay, so we're doing this now.

"I'm really sorry," I say. "I didn't mean for that to happen."

"You didn't mean to use the truth serum on me?" he asks, doubtful. "How is that even possible?"

"No, I did mean to use it," I admit, feeling like an asshole. "I just didn't mean for everything to go down like it did. I was planning on getting you alone and then using it on you so no one else was around and heard what we were talking about. But then I accidentally bumped you, and then you came into the office, and well . . ." I shrug, unsure what else to say. "You know the rest."

"And just how were you planning to get me alone?"

"*Huh?*"

He takes a deliberate step toward me with his eyes on me. "You said you were planning on getting me alone. How were you going to do that?"

"I don't know." I resist the impulse to step back, even though his eyes are super intense right now, like way, way too much to handle intensity. "It wouldn't be that hard. We're alone a lot."

"Not really." The scents of his cologne, soap, and woodsy musk grace my nostrils as he inches closer. "We've been alone maybe twice since the first time I met you."

"We were alone when we first met just outside the club bathroom, when you showed me the morgue"—I count down on my fingers—"in the hallways a couple of times, in the car when we drove to the morgue, when we were in the woods at that zombie's crime scene, when we transported back to the academy . . ." I trail off, noticing how satisfied he appears. "Why are you looking at me like that?"

"It's nothing." He shrugs, but a smile threatens to shine through. "It's just nice to know you're keeping track of the time we've spent together."

I grimace. "Is this payback for using the serum on you?"

He laughs darkly, peering out the window again. "Nope. When I do that, you'll know."

Goose bumps sprout across my arms. "Well, just a heads up, I'm going to be a hard target to take down. I've got a witch for an aunt; I know a ton of Foreseers and Keepers; and all of them have mad connections."

He angles his head forward to get a better look outside. "Who said I was going to use anything magical on you?"

I squirm, feeling way out of my comfort zone. Nothing magical at all? What else is there?

"Well, good luck with that," I say, feigning coolness. When he doesn't say anything, my discomfort switches to frustration. "What're you even looking at out there? Is someone out there?"

"Not anymore." His forehead creases. "But there's trace of fey fog coming out of the forest, and I'm wondering why."

"Oh. I know what it's from."

His head whips in my direction. "You do?"

I nod and quickly tell him about the Empress of the Water Fey and Vivianne wandering out into the forest, which leads to another conversation about why the empress is out, roaming the human world. At first, I don't want to tell him, but he manages to wiggle the truth out of me.

"So, your grandpa's essence is missing, and he made some deal with the Queen of the Underworld to tell your grandma not to look for it?" He sinks onto the bed, the mattress squeaking beneath his weight. "I hate to say this, Alana, but your grandpa's case is getting more complicated by the second. I'm worried it might get taken over by someone higher up. And I haven't reported yet that we found his traveling crystal near a crime scene."

I sit down on the bed beside him. "You're not going to do that yet, right? You said I had a week to look into it."

He runs his hand over his head, making his hair go crazy wild, but in a sexy way. "I don't know." His hand drops to his side. "God, I can't believe the water fey are out of the Underworld. We're going to get calls left and right."

"The Keepers know they're out," I remind him. "They'll keep things in order."

"They might try, but I guarantee there are going to be more murders. We'll probably take on more cases than we can handle. I'm sure I'll have to give some of my older cases to other investigators to take on the new cases coming in." He shakes his head, his leg bouncing up and down with his jitteriness. "If anyone finds out I've been withholding evidence on your grandpa's case..."

I place a hand on his bouncing leg, trying to calm him. "They won't. If anyone questions you about the crystal ball, blame it on me. I'm the one who begged you not to turn it in."

"They'd still blame it on me. I'm the one training you. You're my responsibility."

"All you have to do is go to Vivianne. That woman would be more than happy to put the blame on me."

He frowns. "She does seem to hate you."

"So, will you still give me that week, then?" I ask. "Please, please, pretty please. I'd greatly appreciate it."

He dithers then heaves a defeated sigh. "You have six days left... I'm counting today as one."

"Thank you. I owe you big time." I relax a smidgen. "Seriously, whatever you want, just say the word, and I'll do it for you."

His gaze flits to my hand on his leg. "That's a pretty risky thing to offer."

Pulling my hand away, I give him a hardy-har-har look. "You know what? You and your brother are more alike than you think."

Anger smolders in his eyes. "Dash and I are nothing alike."

"Oh, yeah?" I arch my brows in insinuation. "Because that little pervy remark you just said sounds like something Dash would say."

He grits his teeth. "What exactly did he say to you while he was here?"

"Not much. He joked around a lot and peeked in my underwear drawer. Other than that, we mostly just talked about what Vivianne could be up to. He tried to listen to their conversation, but he said he couldn't hear anything and wondered if maybe

Vivianne has a blocking spell. He said he had some sort of back-up plan to find out what she was up to, but didn't give me the deets." I pause. "Jax, does Dash know about the Electi? I mean, I think he—"

"I need to keep an eye on him," he talks over me, targeting a please-take-the-hint-and-shut-up look. "He has a knack for getting into trouble."

"Yeah, I can tell." I ravel a strand of hair around my finger. "But so do I."

He exaggeratedly nods. "Yes, you definitely do."

"Well, aren't you just Mr. Funny Pants tonight?"

"I was having a pretty good night until I had to play the knight in shining armor for some crazy girl."

"Why? Were you on a hot date or something?"

His gaze bores into me. "Would you be jealous if I was?"

I roll my eyes, like how absurd. "Nope. I don't get jealous."

"Everyone gets jealous, Alana, so I know you're lying." he says.

I point at myself. "Nope. This girl never gets jealous. I'm, like, the opposite of jealous."

"You're such a liar," he says. "And one day, I'm going to prove it."

"Oh, look, another threat." I square my shoulders. "Just prepare yourself for an epic challenge, werewolf dude."

"Oh, I am, and it'll be half the fun." He props his foot on his knee, seeming pretty confident. "And FYI, I was undercover tonight."

"On a date undercover?" Why can't I just let this go? I'm starting to sound more jealous by the second.

"Maybe." His amusement intensifies, but then it fizzles as he goes back to one of our many problems. "You said you saw a wolf outside tonight?"

"Well, I'm not positive it was a wolf," I say. "And I doubt it was a werewolf since it's not a full moon."

He rubs his fingers across his lips, thinking. "Some wolves can change when the moon isn't full."

"Really? How come I've never heard of that?"

"Because not a lot of people know about it."

I chew on my bottom lip, studying his profile, the tension in his jaw. "Can you?"

He shakes his head. "No, but I know a few who can. I'll ask around and see if anyone's heard anything." He won't look me in the eye for some reason, and when he speaks again, he's dropped the wolf subject. "I need to figure out what to do about this Electi problem. I don't understand why they just painted a mark on the floor outside your room and didn't come after you."

He's definitely hiding something. I think of the wolf I saw kill the vampire the day Jax and I first met. Who was the mysterious wolf with silver eyes just like Jax's? He insists it wasn't him, but I'm not convinced just yet. Why would he kill a vampire, though?

"Probably to let me know they're aware I know about them," I say.

He rubs his hand across his jawline. "I feel like there might be more to it than that."

"Like they hid a message in the paint?" I joke.

He straightens, jumps to his feet, and hurries for the door.

"Where are you going?" I rush across the room after him.

"I want to see something." He steps out into the dimly lit hallway and goes into investigator mode, crouching down in front of the mark on the floor.

I glance around at the shut doors lining the wall, making sure no one is around. "What are you looking for?"

He traces across the dry, flaking paint. "It seems strange that they'd just paint the floor and take off. They didn't do that with me."

"How long have you known about them?"

"A couple of months." He aligns his palm to the tile, his brows furrowing.

My jaw nearly smacks the floor. "How have you managed to avoid them for a couple of months?"

His silver eyes sparkle as he glances up at me. "Alana, I'm a werewolf. I have heightened senses and speed. I can be lethal when I need to. It's going to take a lot of manpower and planning to get ahold of me."

"Are they strong? The Electi, I mean? Do they have any powers?"

"Honestly, I don't know a lot about them other than they're cold-blooded murderers." He returns his attention to the painted mark on the floor. "I'm working on finding out more, though." He studies the mark with his head slanted to the side. "Look at how the paint is peeling up. It almost looks like . . ." He squints at the floor.

I crouch down beside him. "Wait a second. There are patterns in the paint."

He bobs his head up and down, tracing his fingertips along the paint. "They're all over it."

I sketch a symbol hidden in the paint and swear a spark of heat surges through me, like static shock. "They look like maybe a language, but I've never seen it before."

"Me, neither." He stands up, retrieves his phone from his pocket, and snaps a photo of the mark. "I might know someone who can translate this for us."

"Really? Who?"

"A friend."

I straighten my legs and stand. "Are you going to tell me who this friend is?"

He deliberates, tilting his head from side to side. "Eventually."

"Speaking of phones, why the heck are you keeping mine

hostage?"

"Not out here," he hisses under his breath, ushering me back into my room.

Once we get inside, he drags the dresser across the room and shoves it front of the door. Then he sends a text and puts away his phone.

"There. No one should be able to get in now." he says, dusting off his hands.

I flop down on my bed and roll onto my stomach. "That's brilliant and everything, but how are you going to get out?"

He starts unbuttoning his shirt. "I'm not."

I prop up on my elbows. "Whoa, whoa, whoa. Why are you undressing?"

Instead of answering me, he undoes button after button then slips his shirt off, revealing a black T-shirt.

"Is that disappointment I sense?" he asks.

I roll my eyes and lie back down. "Nope." My puzzlement increases when he kicks off his boots and removes his belt. "Okay, what's up with the striptease?"

"I'm not giving you a striptease. I'm getting ready for bed." He drops his belt to the floor then approaches the bed, motioning for me to scoot over.

"Are you freaking kidding me?" I aim a finger at my roommate's bed. "If you want to stay, you can sleep there."

He clenches his hands, the muscles of his lean, heavily inked arms rippling. "Would you stop being a pain in the ass and just scoot over? I want to try something."

"Yeah, I've heard that line before," I say yet scoot over, anyway.

Once my back is against the wall, he lies down beside me. The mattress squeaks under his weight as he gets situated in the twin-sized bed, which seems very, very small at the moment. After he gets settled, he pulls the blankets all the way over our heads like a tent.

"Is this where you show me something? Just a warning, if you start undoing your zipper, I'm going to knee you in the balls."

He lets out a frustrated growl. "Oh, my God, you're driving me crazy."

I give him a sugary sweet smile. "The feeling's mutual."

He shakes his head. "Look, I have to stick my hand in my pocket, but you're going to want to see what I have in there."

I decide to drop my awesome jokes for now and zip my mouth shut.

He reaches into his pocket, and what he pulls out causes my heart to leap in my chest.

"A whispering crystal." I gape in awe at the palm-sized crystal crammed with fragments of glittering silver branches that once grew on the whispering tree hidden in the Hushing Forest.

"Impressive, huh?" The shimmering ring of pale purple glowing from the crystal illuminates the smug look on his face.

"Honestly, yeah." I brush my fingers across it, and a spark of magic kisses my fingertips. It's strange since I have no power in me. "These things are really rare . . . How did you get it?"

"Dash stole it from my father. And I confiscated it from him." He pulls a wary expression at the crystal. "I was going to give it back, but I had this feeling it might come in handy one day."

"Why did your father have it to begin with? I thought you said he was a Guardian."

"He is a Guardian. He bought it off some witch to help him on a case once. He never got rid of it, though. He put it on display in our living room. I think he liked to brag that he had it."

I bite my tongue, refusing to comment, no matter how desperately I want to.

"I know what you're thinking," he snaps. "And he's not like

that. He didn't keep it because he's hiding secrets."

"I didn't say that, did I?"

"I can see it all over your face. And no matter what your Keeper parents have taught you, not everyone has a hidden agenda."

"I never said they did." My tone sharpens. "And don't bring my parents into this."

His lips part, ready to blast me with a cruel comeback, but then he fuses his lips together and composes himself. "You know what? I don't have time for this."

I expect him to get up and leave, but he sets the crystal down between us and rotates it until the orb shifts from pale purple to a murky grey. I know enough about the Whispering Crystal to know we can now talk without anyone eavesdropping.

But two questions cross my mind: 1) How the hell did Jax get the crystal to work when only witches are supposed to hold that kind of power? And 2) Who does he think is listening to our conversation?

CHAPTER FOUR

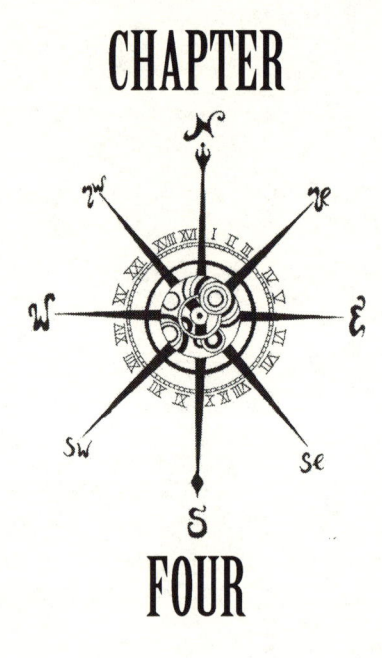

I TAP THE CRYSTAL WITH my finger. "How did you get it to work?"

He shrugs. "I have my ways."

I skeptically eye him over. "Are you hiding a witch's mark somewhere?"

"No," he replies. When I shoot him a skeptical look, he adds, "If you want to search me, then go ahead, but you won't find one."

I lose my mind for a half a second and consider peering under his shirt to see if he's hiding a mark under there, but I manage to keep a firm grasp on my sanity.

"Did you steal a bit of temporary Wicca magic? Because that's the only other reason I can think of."

His lips lift to a small smile. "I'm impressed. I thought it'd take you longer to figure it out."

I lightly prod him in the chest with my finger. "Hey, I know a thing or two about witches. Remember, my aunt's one. I also know that you better hurry up and say whatever you need to say, because you only have a few minutes before that magic wears off."

"I know that." He blows out a breath. "You remember that noise you heard on the phone?"

"The dying alien noise?"

He nods. "I'm pretty sure your phone's been bugged. By whom, I'm not sure. My original guess was the Electi, but it could be a couple of other people, too. I'm going to take it to a friend of mine who can check it out and see."

"But why would anyone want to listen to my conversations?" I ask. "I'm super boring."

"The Electi probably don't think you're boring." He traces his fingers along the edge of the crystal. "I'm also wondering if it might be Vivianne."

"Why would she do that to me? Like I said, I'm super boring." I know the real reason, though. She thinks I have the dagger.

"You sure about that?" he asks, eyeballing me suspiciously. "Or is there something you know that you're not telling me, like maybe the reason Vivianne doesn't like you so much?"

I keep a neutral expression. "Well, she hates Keepers, and pretty much my entire family belongs to the group."

"She doesn't think too highly of your grandpa, either," he points out. "And he wasn't a Keeper."

I force down the pain and sadness threatening to choke me. "Most people don't think too highly of him right now."

"Alana, I can't help you if you don't tell me everything. I know there's more to this than you're letting on." His intense gaze burrows into me. "When Vivianne called you into the office that day you found out your grandpa died, you came out looking angry and upset."

"I just found out my grandpa died." My voice cracks. "How else was I supposed to look?"

"Upset, but not angry." He waits, as if expecting me to confess. But I can't tell him about the dagger. If I do, then I'm admitting that my grandpa is guilty of stealing it. I can't do that, not until I find out the reason he took it.

"If we're going to be partners, we have to start trusting each other," he presses. "Please, just tell me what you know."

"Partners?" I elevate my brows. "I thought you were only training me."

"You know what I mean. I'm just trying to make a point that, if we're going to be working together, we have to trust each other. Working on murder cases can get really dangerous." He carries my gaze, pressing the severity. "I think the mark outside your door proves that."

"What are we going to do about that mark? If someone wakes up and sees it—"

"Don't change the subject. I want to know what's going on with you and Vivianne."

Hmmm . . . Do I dare tell him about the dagger? Can I trust him?

He might be the only one . . . Just be careful . . . Don't tell him where . . . you hid . . . it . . . Grandpa's voice fades.

I sigh tiredly, wishing he would stop disappearing on me and tell me the full truth.

"It's about the Dagger of Conspectu . . . Vivianne thinks my grandpa stole it right before he died."

"Yeah, I know she does."

"How?"

He lifts a shoulder to give a half-shrug, which looks awkward while he's lying on his side. "She told me."

"Oh."

"But is that all she said to you."

"Maybe," I say, heavy with indecision. When he shoots me a fess-up look, I cave. "I'll tell you, but you have to promise not to tell Vivianne."

He easily nods. "I've never trusted the woman, but the fact that she just wandered into the forest with the Empress of the Water Fey . . ." He shakes his head, his expression hardening. "Let's just say I'll be very careful about what information I divulge to her."

I swallow down my nerves and cross my fingers I'm not making a huge, epic mistake. "She thinks he gave the dagger to me before he died and that I still have it."

"And do you?"

I stare at the glowing crystal between us, the light blinding, yet I don't blink. "Maybe."

Silence encases us, and my heart beats deafeningly inside my chest. God, I hope I can trust him.

"Where is it?" he finally asks.

I bring my gaze to him and put on a determined face. "Someplace safe."

He opens and flexes his hand. "You're not going to tell me, are you?"

I offer him an apologetic look. "No. I can't. Sorry."

He frowns. "I just hope you really did put it someplace safe."

"I did. And it's protected by magic, so it should be hard to find."

"Good." He props up on his arm and rests his chin against his hand. "Is there anything else you need to tell me?"

Other than I hear my dead grandpa's voice in my head? "Nope. But I have a question for you."

He casts a fleeting glance at the crystal. The light is fading. We're running low on time.

"Make it quick."

"I just want to know why Dash isn't being targeted by the Electi," I blurt out. "When he was in the office, he heard everything you said while you were on the Truth Serum, so doesn't he know what they are?"

The crystal reflects against his eyes and highlights his apprehension. "He does know, has for a while, actually."

My eyes pop wide. *"Really?"*

He nods, shifting his weight forward and moving closer to me. "But no one knows he knows . . . and probably never will."

"Why? What is he?" I ask, hoping he doesn't dodge the question this time.

He stiffens, and I worry he's not going to tell me.

"Because . . . Dash has certain gifts that make . . . that make it almost impossible for someone to track down an identity on him." He watches, waiting to see if I can put two and two together.

"Wait a minute . . ." Realization clicks. "Are you saying he's a shapeshifter?"

"Not quite, but he has shapeshifting skills, which makes him really hard to track down." His tone carries an edge.

"How can he have shapeshifting skills but not be a shapeshifter?" After all, from everything I know, no other creature can shapeshift.

His lips part right as the crystal dims out. Blackness engulfs us. The air stills between us.

"You should probably get to sleep," he presses in a firm tone.

I catch his underlying meaning. No more talking about Dash or anything Electi related.

But why can't I talk about Dash? What on earth is he? And why doesn't Jax want people to know?

CHAPTER FIVE

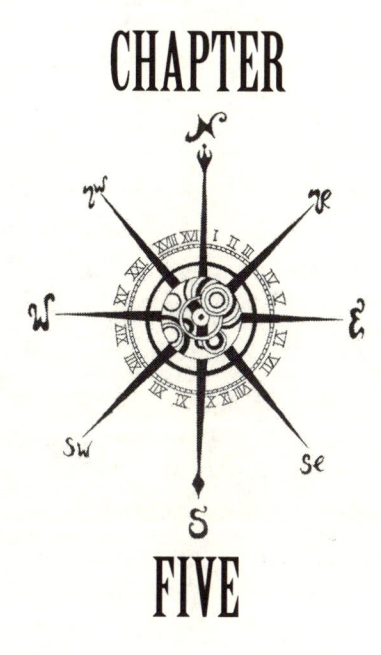

I'M HAVING THE BEST NIGHTMARE-FREE dream for the first time since I got my mark when I'm startled awake by an annoyingly loud ringing.

My eyelids lift, and sunlight instantly blinds me as a faint, woodsy, wolfish scent engulfs my nostrils. At first, I'm like, who the heck am I all cuddled up with? Then I remember last night and how Jax never left my bed before I fell sleep.

Rubbing the sleepiness from my eyes, I start to sit up to answer the phone that won't shut up, but then I freeze, realizing the position Jax and I are in. Not only did we sleep together in the same bed, but my head is resting on the crook of his lean arm, my hand is on his rock solid waist, and my leg is hitched over his.

Is this why I slept so well last night?

I shake the ridiculous thought from my head. *Stop, Alana,*

just stop.

I carefully lift my hand off his abs, slide my leg away from his, and slowly sit up. My gaze drops to Jax, and I breathe in relief. He's still fast asleep. Thank God. If he would've woken up, I'd never have heard the end of it.

The phone continues to ring as I study him. He's resting on his back with his lips slightly parted, and his hair a crazy mess, but in a sexy way that makes me want to run my fingers through the strands to see how soft they are. I keep my insanity in check, though, and resist the crazy compulsion.

God, what would he think if he knew what I was thinking?

"Sleep well last night?" Jax murmurs with his eyes closed and a faint smile tickling his lips.

Dammit! How long has he been awake?

"No, not really," I lie through a yawn. "I actually had a ton of nightmares of some stalker sneaking into bed with me."

His eyelids open, and a grin breaks across his face. "You do realize you let me sleep in your bed, right?"

I narrow my eyes at him. "Just because I fell asleep before you did, it doesn't mean I wouldn't have kicked you out."

"You're such a liar." He tucks his arms behind his head with a ghost of a smirk on his lips. "You felt too safe to kick me out."

"I'm not a damsel in distress; I can take care of myself."

"You may not be a damsel in distress, but you definitely need a babysitter. You're a handful."

"Hey, I totally took care of myself before you came into my life." I pause, deciding if I want to go where my thoughts are headed. "But I'm very grateful that you stayed with me last night and didn't let anyone try to kill me in my sleep."

"Wow. Did I just get a thank you . . . ?" He trails off as the phone rings again.

Sitting up, he digs his phone out of his pocket and hammers his finger against the talk button. "This is Jax." He remains quiet, listening, and then his gaze slides to me. "Okay, but I have to bring my trainee." He pauses. "Because she's under strict orders not to be left alone." Another pause. "Well, she can make up her class work on the weekend." Irritation flickers in his eyes. "Fine, I'll let her know." He hangs up, drops his phone onto his lap, and runs his hand across his face. "We got called into a case."

"*We?*" I question. "Since when do I go on cases?"

He lowers his hand from his face and throws me a *"really"* look. "Since you decided to go digging around into stuff you shouldn't." He tosses off the blankets, rises to his feet, and stretches his arms above his head.

"I think we already established that I don't need a babysitter," I say, doing my best not to gawk at his lean ab muscles peeking out from the hem of his black T-shirt.

An arrogant smile tugs at his lips. "Enjoying the view?"

"Nope, not at all." I feel stupid for getting busted, though not enough to blush. "And how am I supposed to go on a case with you when I have detention? Don't get me wrong; I'd way rather spend a day looking at dead bodies than hanging out in *her* office, doing stacks of homework, and then cleaning the bathrooms with the janitor, but I don't think she's going to be all for it."

"She made you clean the *bathrooms?*"

I nod, kicking the rest of the blankets off me and sitting up. "And it sucked balls. I mean, Henry's a cool dude and everything, but the guys' bathroom reeks almost as bad as an outhouse."

Shaking his head, he scoops up his shirt from off the floor. "She shouldn't make you do that. It's against the rules."

I scoot to the edge of the bed and lower my feet to the cold linoleum floor. "I don't think she really cares about rules."

He slips his arms through the sleeves of his shirt. "She may think she doesn't, but she will after I report both incidents."

I comb my fingers through my long, brown, tangled hair. "I

thought you couldn't report her because she's the person you're supposed to report stuff, too. That's what Dash said last night."

"I'll go to the Guardian committee." He does up a button on his shirt. "They should be able to take care of it."

"The Guardian committee?" I crinkle my nose. "Aren't they supposed to be very strict and by the books kind of people?"

He finishes buttoning up his shirt then reaches for his belt on the floor. "They are, but that's a good thing. They'll be more hard on her."

"I guess I see your point." I rub the dreariness from my eyes, push to my feet, and wander to my dresser to get some clean clothes. "So, why didn't Dash mention the committee last night?"

He loops the belt through his jeans. "Probably because our father's on it, and they don't really get along."

I pull open the top dresser drawer. "Yeah, I kind of picked up on that last night."

He freezes in the middle of doing up the belt buckle, and his questioning gaze elevates to me. "Dash talked to you about our father?"

"He just mentioned him a couple of times, and I could sense there was some tension." I take out a black tank top, jeans, and a plaid shirt and then bump the dresser drawer shut. "He also said something when I first met him about you being brainwashed by your father."

"Yeah, I forgot he said that." He flattens his hand over his head, smoothing his hair with a deep frown etched into his face.

"Everything okay?" I ask cautiously.

He nods, blinking up at me. "Yeah, everything's fine. I just need to go check up on a few things." He hurriedly slips on his boots then backs toward the door without tying the laces. "Meet me out front in ten minutes. Make sure to keep your phone on you at all times. And do not go anywhere else. I mean it, Alana. Nowhere else."

"Yes, sir," I say with a salute. "But when you say nowhere else, does that include the bathroom? Because I really have to pee."

He stares at me, unimpressed. "Yes, you're allowed to go to the bathroom." His tolerant expression goes *poof* as a haughty grin curls at his lips. "But, now that you've called me sir, I really think you should keep—"

"No, thank you," I quickly say, shooing him toward the door. "Now get out. I need to get dressed."

Chuckling, he turns for the door and reaches for the doorknob . . .

Wait a second . . .

I gape at the intact door. "When did the door get fixed?"

"I had someone take care of it last night," he answers, opening the door and revealing that the tile floor is now mark-free.

My lips part in shock. "And the—"

"Would you relax?" He presses me with a shush look, sticking his hand into his front pocket. "Everything's taken care of, so stop worrying."

I nod and keep my lips sealed.

When he removes his hand from his pocket, his fingers are curled around my phone. He gives it back to me and heads for the door again. *"Be careful with what you say,"* he mouths then walks out and shuts the door.

I rush up and twist the lock, hoping that will be enough to keep me safe for the next ten minutes.

CHAPTER SIX

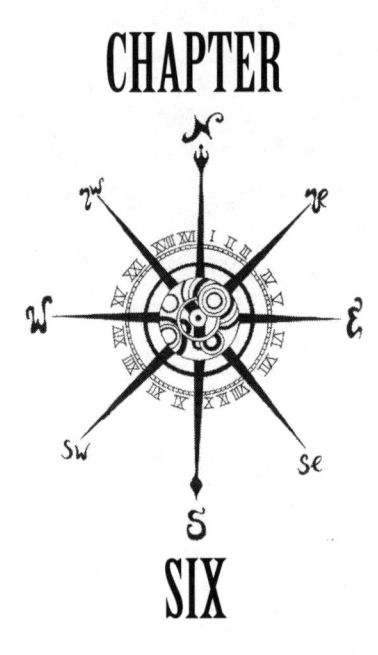

TEN MINUTES LATER, I'M STANDING in front of the school with a gentle morning breeze kissing my skin and the pale pink glow of the sunrise shining down on me. I keep walking up and down the short flight of steps to get my blood pumping and wake myself up more. While I'm not a necessarily exhausted, I've never been a morning person and usually don't fully wake up until I drink a cup of coffee or two. Unfortunately, the cafeteria's coffee tastes like ass.

I stifle a yawn as I jog back up to the top of the stairs and glance down the driveway, searching for Jax's car. Where is he? He's only a few minutes late, but he doesn't seem like a guy who has ever been tardy to anything. It's not like I miss him or anything—okay, maybe a little—but with it being so early, hardly anyone's around, and the aloneness vibe makes me feel squirrely.

I can't stop tossing nervous glances at the trees, plagued by the sense that someone or something is watching me. I consider calling or texting my dad and letting him know about Vivianne's secret meeting with the Empress of the Water Fey, not only to update him on what's going on, but to distract myself from the queasy feeling knotting in the pit of my stomach. But Jax warned me to be careful with what I said over the phone, and I'm guessing that subject falls into the off-limits category.

I thrum my fingers against the sides of my legs as I trot backward up the stairway with my gaze on the trees. *Just relax. It's broad daylight. Nothing's going to happen.*

As if to taunt my optimism, the wind kicks up and tosses dry leaves and dirt in the air. I shield my eyes with my hand and strain to see through the debris and into the woods. I feel myself being pulled, drawn by an unseen force, magnetized to the trees . . . or something that lies beyond them . . .

My feet begin to move. I take each step robotically. The wind dances more vibrantly. I swear I hear a plea for help . . .

Help us . . .

Help . . .

My phone rings from inside my pocket, jerking me out of the strange trance, only to realize the wind isn't blowing, and the leaves on the dirt and grass appear untouched.

What on earth? Did I just imagine it happening?

The uneasiness in my gut magnifies as I dig out my phone. Figuring it's Jax telling me he's going to be late, I answer without checking the screen.

"What's up with the tardiness, wolf dude?" I answer, gripping the side railing with my attention on the trees.

Everything seems so quiet now.

"Alana?" my mom's voice fills the line.

"Oh, sorry." I sink down onto a step, prop my elbow on my knee, and rest my chin in my hand. Hearing her voice brings an instant comfort to me, and the tension in my body mildly reduces. "I thought you were Jax."

"Oh . . . Do you talk to him a lot?" Her tone is mixed with concern and curiosity. I can already see where her thoughts are heading.

"Kind of, but only because he's training me. And that's the *only* reason."

"Okay." She doesn't sound too convinced. "But if you ever want to talk to me about anything, even a guy you like or maybe you're dating, you can talk to me."

"Thanks, but I don't like anyone at the moment, and I am definitely not dating anyone." Especially since no one at this school can stand the sight of me.

Ever since my grandpa died and was accused of horrible things, no one wants to associate with me. I've gotten into multiple fights and gotten detention for fighting, even though I never started the fights and was only trying to defend myself.

"Is everything okay, sweetie?" my mom asks. "You sound upset."

"I'm fine." I'm not about to tell her the truth about what's going on. She's been through too much over the last week. "I'm just tired."

"You should get some more rest, then. I'm actually surprised you answered the phone. You usually don't get up this early."

"Jax and I got called in to a case, or else I would be in bed."

"A case? Wow. I didn't know they let first years do that."

"They usually don't, but Jax wanted to take me with him this time. I guess he thought it'd be a good learning experience." Another lie, but the last thing I want to do is bring her into this mess. The more in the dark she is, the better.

"Well, good. I hope you're having fun or at least aren't as upset as you were when you first got your mark." Worry creeps into her tone. "I just hope you aren't overworking yourself."

"I'm not. I promise." I rise to my feet as I spot Jax's blue and black striped 1967 Pontiac GTO turning into the driveway. "Hey, Mom, I have to go. I'll talk to you later, okay?"

"Okay, sweetie. I just wanted to call and make sure you were okay," she says. "And to let you know that, if you ever need to talk, I'm here."

I pause mid-step. "Is everything okay with you? You sound—I don't know—worried."

"I'm fine," she insists. "There's just a lot going on with this whole water fey ordeal. I swear to God, faeries can be such a pain in the ass sometimes."

"Yeah, I know." Dammit, I wish I could tell her about last night! "Maybe after you and Dad save the world this time, you should take a vacation."

"Yeah, that sounds nice," she agrees. "Maybe one on the beach out on some remote island."

"You two definitely deserve it." I trot down the rest of the steps as Jax parks at the curb in front of the stairway. "Okay, I've really got to go this time. I'll call you later."

"Okay," she says. "I love you. And Dad says he loves you, too."

"Tell him I love him, too." I reach for the car door handle. "Love you, Mom. Bye."

When she says good-bye back, I cast one final glance at the seemingly peaceful forest before climbing into the car. The smell of coffee, cologne, and vanilla air freshener instantly graces my nostrils.

"I didn't peg you for being a late kind of guy," I joke as I fasten my seatbelt and settle back in the leather seat.

He has changed into another black T-shirt and matching combat boots, and his hair is styled messily. He seems irritated, too—well, more irritated than normal.

"I had a couple of errands to run that took longer than I

expected." He shifts into drive, pulls out onto the highway that weaves through the woodsy mountains, and then nods at two thermoses in the open middle console. "I brought you coffee."

I pick up one of the thermoses. "Wow, that was sweet of you. What's the occasion?"

He shrugs with his eyes fixed on the road. "It's just coffee."

Okay, so Mr. Grumpy Pants has definitely returned.

I prepare myself for a blast of staleness as I bring the cup to my mouth, figuring he probably got the coffee from the cafeteria. But the delicious, warm liquid that nearly melts my taste buds definitely isn't crappy cafeteria coffee.

"Oh, my God, where did you get this?" I take another sip, and a soft moan escapes my lips. "It tastes amazing."

He shrugs, glancing at me, his gaze briefly flicking to my lips. "I made it."

I gape at him. "You made this?"

"Yeah," he says with another shrug. "It's not a big deal. It's just a cup of coffee."

"It is, too, a big deal. I haven't had a good cup of coffee in weeks. The cafeteria's tastes so bad it made me want to throw up." I raise the thermos to my mouth and bask in another sip. "This, though . . . This is heaven." I move my nose over the steam and inhale. Oh. My. God. It even smells good. "You should bring me a cup of this every day."

"Every day?" He cocks a brow. "That sounds like a lot of work for someone I can barely tolerate."

"Hey!" I mock being offended, pressing my hand to my heart. "How can you say that? I thought we were best friends." When he gives me an unimpressed look, I sigh. "Fine. Don't bring me a cup of coffee every morning. Ruin my dream of living in coffee heaven." I sip my coffee, relaxing back in the seat.

Silence stretches between us as he cruises down the road, fiddling with the radio and heater, growing more fidgety with each mile marker we pass. While he's not a skip-through-the-rainbows-and-smile sort of guy, a dark cloud of gloom seems to hover over his head.

"Are you all right?" I finally ask. "You seem kind of—I don't know—pissed off about something."

"I'm fine." He reaches for the other thermos. "I'm just thinking about this case we're going to."

"Okay." *Vague much?* "What about the case is bugging you? Because you seem bugged about something."

"That's the thing. I don't know anything about it. Usually, my supervisor gives me a brief rundown over the phone so I know what I'm getting into, but this time, she said she couldn't, that I'd have to wait until I got there. That's never happened before."

"Maybe she was too busy or something."

"No, it wasn't that. She sounded . . . nervous." He wraps his fingers around the shifter. "Maybe it was a bad idea to bring you."

My grip constricts around the mug. "Why? I've already been to, like, three murder scenes, including one where a zombie was dragged behind a car, and some of his rotting flesh had melted into the pavement." I shiver at the mental image. "How much worse could this one be?"

"The very fact that you asked that shows how bad of an idea this is." He rakes his fingers through his hair. "I just didn't want you being alone all day."

I set the coffee between my legs. "I'm going to be alone eventually. You can't watch me 24/7."

A challenge dances in his eyes. "Wanna bet?"

"Jax, you can't go everywhere with me." I grimace. "I need privacy sometimes so I can do private things."

His eyes glisten with intrigue. "What kind of private things?"

"Nothing you get to know about," I retort with a sassy grin.

"And you want to know why? Because you're not going to be with me all the time."

"I know I'm not, but someone is." He's being so relentless.

I open my mouth to protest, but he talks over me.

"Alana, this isn't a joke. What happened last night . . . This is really fucking bad. These people don't mess around. Whatever they did last night has a purpose, and until I can figure out what they're up to, I'm not letting you go anywhere unprotected."

"I know it's not a joke, but I know how to defend myself." I pick up the coffee to take another drink. "I'm not helpless."

"I know you're not helpless," he says, seeming genuine, "but I also don't feel comfortable letting you be by yourself when the people who cause at least seventy percent of the murders are after you."

I go all bug-eyed. "*Seventy* percent?"

He nods. "And that's just the ones we manage to solve. I don't even want to think about how many cold cases are connected to them."

I gulp down a long drink of coffee, letting reality sink in. I spent most of my life living in a world filled with danger and have put myself in dangerous positions on multiple occasions. This, though . . . This is undeniably the worst situation I've ever been in. But I'm not about to be a coward and hide out in my room.

"I think I need to get some weapons," I announce, putting the thermos back between my legs.

His brows knit. "Why?"

"So I can protect myself." I trace my finger around the lid of the thermos. "It'll have to be an inconspicuous weapon—no swords or bows or anything like that. Maybe a knife or a Taser. Or maybe I can get my parents to get me a knife laced with siren blood. That's supposed to be really lethal to almost every creature out there."

"You can't have a weapon on school grounds. If you get caught, you'll probably be expelled."

"If the Electi catch me unarmed, I'll probably die."

He reaches over and puts a finger against my lips. "Try to refrain from saying their name as much as possible. You don't want anyone to overhear you."

"Sorry," I mumble, my lips moving against his finger. "I'm just trying to come up with a plan."

"I know." He withdraws his finger from my mouth as he mulls something over. "Let me get you a weapon. I'll make sure to pick something out that you can carry with you at all times but will be easy to keep hidden."

"*You're* going to pick me out a weapon?"

"Yes. And when I give the weapon to you, you're going to apologize for questioning my weapon competency."

"Sounds good to me, but just so you know, I'm pretty hard to impress when it comes to weapons."

Instead of responding, he gives me an overconfident smile then redirects his attention to the road. "So, here's the rules for when we get to the crime scene. Under no circumstances are you to leave my side unless I tell you to. Don't touch anything unless I give you permission. And try not to get too snarky with my supervisor. She won't be as tolerant as I am."

A thousand comebacks tickle at the tip of my tongue, but all of them die the instant Jax presses on the brake to slow down for a string of cars parked around a dry field.

"Is this the crime scene?" I ask, straightening in the seat.

He nods, silencing the engine. "Yep, this is it."

"But it's so close to the academy." I crane my neck to get a better look as I undo my seatbelt. My view is limited by SUVs, cars, and people dressed in similar attire as Jax.

"I know." Fear briefly flickers in his silver eyes, but he quickly composes himself. "It's actually happened a few times over the last six months or so."

I set the coffee back in the console. "You don't think it has anything to do with the academy, do you?"

"There's been some speculation that it might." He extends his hand toward the door handle. "I'll explain everything later. Right now, we have a case to investigate."

When he gets out of the car and closes the door, I follow his lead, meeting him around the front of the car.

"So, where do we start first?" I ask, tying my plaid shirt around my waist.

"We go look at the damage." He draws on his sunglasses and starts off toward the dry, grassy field.

I trail at his heels, noting the way people keep glaring at me, probably because I'm a newbie and am technically not supposed to be here.

"Stay close to me," Jax utters from under his breath as we reach the outskirts of the field where the pavement meets the grass and dirt. "And remember, don't touch anything."

I'm starting to nod when my grandpa's voice fills my head.

Brace yourself, Alana, he whispers. *It's about to start.*

Confusion spins inside me. The feeling only lasts a spilt second before an overwhelming wave of despair crashes through me, so powerful I nearly drop to my knees.

Fearing I'm about to collapse, I clutch Jax's arm.

His eyes drop to my fingers digging into his bicep then rise to my face, his brows furrowing. "What's wrong?"

Tears sting my eyes. "I think something's . . ." I trail off as I catch sight of the field in front of me. The once dry, yellow grass is now stained red with spilled blood, and lifeless, dismembered fey stretch as far as my eyes can see. And the stench. God, the stench . . . It's like spoiled meat left out for days to rot in the sunlight.

Vomit burns the back of my throat, but the nausea is

suffocated by the sound of voices blasting through me like exploding glass.

Help us!
Help me!
I can't breathe!
Why are you doing this!
What did we do!
I don't want to die!
I don't want to die.
I don't . . .
Want to . . .
Die . . .

CHAPTER SEVEN

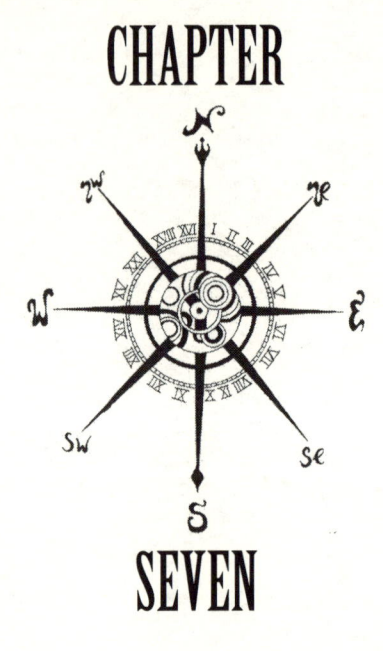

MY HEAD PULSATES MADDENINGLY, AS if my brain is fighting to escape my skull, fighting to escape the voices. Faint whispers haunt my thoughts then gradually fade like a light mist.

Help . . .

Please . . . I . . . don't . . . want . . . to . . . die . . . The last voice slips from my grasp as I return to reality, and the pain in my head subsides.

"Alana." Jax's alarmed face is the first thing that comes into focus. "What the heck just happened?"

"I, um . . ." I blink several times, attempting to piece together what happened, but I have absolutely no idea other than maybe a spirit entered me. It seemed different than that, though. More powerful. Like an army of spirits all screamed at me simultaneously. "Jax, I think something's . . ."

Not here, my grandpa whispers. *There are too many wandering ears around.*

I scan the people around me and note that many are watching me like a hawk.

I quickly wipe the tears from my eyes. "I'm sorry," I tell Jax. "It's just a lot to take in."

"Yeah, it is." He presses his lips together with an unreadable expression on his face. "Are you sure you want to do this? It's a lot to handle, especially for someone so inexperienced."

"I'm fine," I assure him. "I can handle it."

I'm not sure if I can, and deep down, I want nothing more than to hide out in the car, away from the pain, blood, and evidence of evil. But every fiber in my being is pulling me toward that field. It's the exact same feeling I experienced when I was sitting outside the school this morning. Was it merely a coincidence? Or did I somehow sense that, a handful of miles away, a massacre had happened?

Jax doesn't seem to buy into my chillaxed act, but he doesn't push the matter further.

"All right, come on." He nods at me to follow as he walks farther into the crime scene.

I tail him, matching his steps to avoid ruining evidence as we make our way down a flattened, body-free section of the field.

The foul stench of death still possesses the air. I want to draw my shirt over my nose, but I don't want to appear uneasy, either.

"Still doing, okay?" Jax asks, glancing left and right at the piles of bodies beside us.

"Yeah, I'm fine." My voice quivers as a pounding urge to touch the bodies burns inside me. The feeling makes me sick to my stomach. What is wrong with me? Why is my mind suddenly so possessed with such morbidly twisted thoughts?

I hug my arms around myself and continue following Jax. *One foot in front of the other. You'll be fine. Just don't look down.*

That's all I want to do: look down and assess the damage. Could it be a Guardian thing? Could my powers, or whatever the hell you want to call them, be expanding?

I fight the compulsion to look down for as long as I can, but when Jax grinds to a halt, I stop with him, and my gaze descends.

The urge takes over, the need to touch the bodies so overpowering I can scarcely breathe.

"I need to go talk to my supervisor for a second and get caught up," he says, skimming the area. "Wait here for a second."

I nod dazedly as he wanders off. When he's far enough away, I bend down and brush my fingers along the arm of a female a few years older than me.

When fey are alive, they mostly remain in their human form. But after they die, the glamour fades, and their original form shows through. Some of their forms are ghastly and terrifying, as bad as scenes in nightmares. Others, though, are hauntingly beautiful. The fey in front of me is part of the latter with shimmering violet skin, silver hair dipped in diamonds, lips tattooed with curvy, inky patterns.

Feel me, a melodious voice floats through my head. *Feel my death...*

Dizziness swims in my brain as her death seeps through my body... The pain... It's unbearable... as hot as lightning yet as cold as a blizzard. I can barely breathe as images flicker through my mind. A tug kisses at my fingertips. I swear I fall... fall into her... become her... die with her.

"We shouldn't be here," I say as I stand in the middle of the field surrounded by my fellow fey. My violet skin sparkles in the pale moonlight, my silver hair whips in the wind, and a scorching hot power blazes through my veins. "This is a trap."

The man in front of me turns toward me, brushing a lock of his inky black hair out of his crystal blue eyes. "Adaliya, you need to calm down. We have a truce with the Lord of the Afterlife, and he wouldn't dare break that."

I laugh hollowly. "You really think that's true? That the Lord cursed with darkness in his veins wouldn't screw you over?"

"Do I need to remind you who I am?" His threat rumbles from his chest. "Unlike you, I'm not some mere civilian fey. Royal blood pumps through my veins. Remember your place, Adaliya."

Anger simmers under my skin, but I lower my head into a bow. "Yes, sir. I'm just nervous. With the water fey roaming the world now, I'm worried that everything is going to change, that truces might be broken and new ones formed."

"I understand your concern, but I assure you the Lord of the Afterlife would not dare do anything to break the truce with the fey." He towers over me. "We're too powerful."

I internally sigh. The Prince of the North Kingdom is too arrogant for his own good. I should have followed my gut instinct and stayed in the Fey Realm tonight in the safety of our magic.

"You said the Lord sent a letter for us to meet him here tonight," I proceed with caution, choosing my words carefully to avoid angering him more. "But what exactly did he promise that made you so easily break the laws of leaving your kingdom?"

"He said he found the Branch of Eternity." He casts a glance up at the night sky now hazed with clouds. "He wants to make a bargain for it." His eyes land back on me. "Do you know what that would mean for our kind? It would free us from death forever."

"We already live too long as it is," I say. "Not everyone wants to live forever."

"Well, I do, and that's all that matters." He turns his back on me, leaving me to stew in my frustration.

How dare he bring our army out here and risk our lives, all so he can have immortality! He doesn't even know if the letter is actually from the Lord of the Afterlife.

I start to turn away, ready to disobey rules and walk away from this, when a low, grumbling sound rises from the trees. I strain my eyes against the darkness and make out the shadows of human-like figures with red, glowing eyes.

"Eyes of the blood thirsty ones," I whisper in horror. I reach for the prince to warn him, but a scream shatters through the air.

Blurry figures zip out from the trees, moving so fast my eyes can barely keep up. The scent of rust floods the land, and the ground below me softens like mud. At first, I think that maybe it started to rain, but when I glance down, I realize the dirt is soaked in blood.

A gasp escapes my lips as I trip back, reaching for my dagger in my sheath, but a figure zooms toward me and slams their hands against my chest. The dagger falls from my hands as I stumble to the ground, landing on the bodies of my fallen friends.

Dead. Everyone's dead.

A sob wrenches from my chest as I extend my arm to the side and feel around for my weapon. Blood coats my fingers, and tears stain my cheeks.

"No. This can't be happening."

"But it is." A deathly, emotionless face appears above me. Her skin is as pale as the moon, her hair as black as the sky, and her teeth as sharp as my missing dagger.

"You're a vampire." My voice trembles as I lean back, my fingers tracing the ground, searching for my dagger.

"Wow. You're a sharp one," she ridicules with a smirk before wrapping her fingers loosely around my neck and leaning in. "I guess fey were never really known for their intelligence, though, were they?"

"But we were here to meet the Lord of the Afterlife."

"Did you really believe that?" She laughs. "How stupid of you."

I want to tell her she's wrong, want to be confident and strong, but fear overwhelms me, and I only manage to get one word out. "Why?"

"Why?" She hovers closer, so close I can smell the stench of blood staining her pierced lips. "That's the best you can come up with?"

My fingers graze the handle of my dagger, and a drop of hope rises in my chest. "What else am I supposed to ask?"

Her smile widens, blood dripping down her chin. "How about this?" She leans closer, putting her lips to my ear. "Who?"

My fingers fold around the metal handle. "But I already know the answer. It's right in front of me."

She laughs wickedly, the sound sending a chill down my spine. "Stupid fey. Nothing is ever that simple." She slants away from me, raising her head into the moonlight, her lips parting, her fangs ready to sink into my flesh and rip me to bits.

That's when I spot the sequence of symbols branded into her throat.

"You're from one of the facilities," I whisper, inching my dagger close. "This isn't you. This is them, the Electi. They did this to you."

Anger flares in her eyes. "The facilities have done nothing to me except bring out what I truly am!" she roars, her fangs lengthening as she throws her head back.

A trail of moonlight spills across her bloody throat and collarbone. In the hollow of her throat, inked into her flesh, is a tattoo of a blood droplet with a silvery T carved into the center. She's part of the territory clan that lives near Virginia Beach by the coastline. Usually, territory vampires are less violent and more in control of their blood thirst.

It hast to be because of the facilities. They ruined her, just like they're ruining everything else.

I bring my dagger up, aiming it at her chest, but she captures my arm and digs her nails into my flesh.

I wince in pain, the weapon slipping from my fingers as her fangs sink into my neck and split open my throat.

I'm dying . . .

I really am . . .

CHAPTER EIGHT

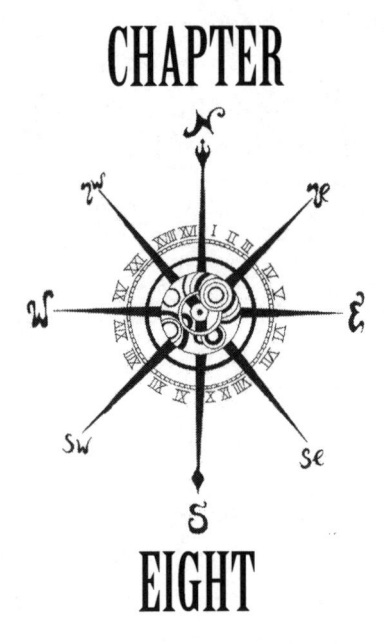

"**W**ELL, JAX, I HAVE TO say, you really picked a winner here," an unfamiliar voice says. "Fainting at the scene? I think that might be a first."

"It's not a first, and you know it. Over half the newbies faint when they see their first real crime scene," Jax replies with a deafening exhale. "And, if I'm remembering correctly, you were one of them."

I want to open my eyes and see who she is, see where I am, but I'm afraid. Cold.

Terrified.

"You're right. I did." The woman's voice turns flirty. "But I'm surprised you remember that."

"How could I forget?" Jax replies. "I'm the one who caught you and saved your ass from smacking the pavement."

She laughs. "Well, I guess you were just paying me back early for all the times I've saved that cute, little butt of yours."

I wait for Jax to respond, but he doesn't. Instead, warm fingers spread across my cheeks.

"Alana, open your eyes." His breath seeps into my skin and thaws the deathly coldness inside me. "Please. You're really starting to worry me."

I don't want to open my eyes at all. I don't want to see the bodies on the ground, bodies I just saw die with my own eyes. How did I see through the eyes of the dead faerie, though? Maybe I'm becoming a Foreseer and am just tapping into my powers? Although, from everything I know, seeing through the dead's eyes isn't a Foreseer trait.

I wait for my grandpa's voice to show up in my mind and tell me if I'm correct or not, but all I hear is the memory of the screams as the fey fell to their painful deaths.

Not knowing what else to do, I open my eyes and return to reality.

The sky is the first thing to come into focus, followed by Jax's face. His sunglasses are drawn to the top of his head, so I get a clear view of the worry flooding his eyes.

"Thank God." A relieved breath eases from his lips, but worry resides in his eyes as he remains crouched beside me with his hands cupping my face. "Are you okay? You fell pretty hard when you fainted."

I want to tell him that I didn't faint, but I zip my lips shut when I become highly aware we have an audience.

The woman standing behind him offers me a stiff smile. She looks a few years older than me with shoulder-length black hair streaked with a bit of red. Like Jax, she's dressed head to toe in black; only, her outfit includes slacks and a business jacket.

"Glad to see there's no permanent damage," she tells Jax as she types something into her phone.

"We don't know if there's any permanent damage," he tells her, leaning closer to examine me. "She could have a concussion. I think I should take her to the doctor."

"I'm fine." I force him to move back and let go of my face as I sit up. The field and trees around me sway with my movements, and my stomach churns as the scent of death assaults my nostrils again. "I don't have a concussion."

"You don't know that for sure," he says, sweeping strands of my hair out of my eyes. "You need to get checked out."

"I'm fine," I insist. Then, to prove it, I stand to my feet. "See? Perfectly fine."

He stands up, too, his gaze trained on me. "Are you sure? Because I'm okay with taking you to the doctor. The academy's not that far away. It'll only take a few minutes—"

"Jax, if she says she's fine, then I'm sure she's fine," the woman interrupts. "And if she does have a concussion, there's not much to be done."

"Yeah, I guess so." He seems torn, his gaze flicking up and down my body as if expecting injuries to suddenly materialize. "But I think she should go wait in the car while I finish up here."

"That's fine with me." The woman turns to me with a stiff smile and offers her hand for me to shake. "I'm Hadlee, by the way. Jax's supervisor."

I inconspicuously eye her over. Is she just a Guardian, or does she have other marks on her? It's hard to tell without actually seeing the marks, but her skin does feel noticeably cold. "It's nice to meet you. I'm Alana . . . but you probably already know that."

"I did." She lets go of my hand, her smile softening as she twists toward Jax. "Check in with me before you leave, okay?"

He nods, his attention still fixed on me. "Yeah, yeah, I know the drill."

She steals another glance at me and frowns before turning

and hiking down the field.

"I think she likes you," I tell Jax after Hadlee is out of earshot.

"She might," he says, watching me closely. "Does that bother you?"

I roll my eyes, but the movement makes my head throb. I bring my fingers to my temple, wincing.

His expression plummets. "Alana, I really don't think you're fine. When you fainted, you—"

"I didn't faint," I whisper. "I . . ." *I, what, Alana? You don't even know what happened.* "I think I need some fresh air."

Without looking at the dead bodies, I make my way back to the road. I figure Jax will stay behind and finish up his job, but instead, he follows me down the path to his car.

I climb into the passenger seat without saying a word, flip down the visor, and cringe at my reflection in the small mirror. Blood marks scuff my cheeks, jawline, and neck, painfully reminding me of how it felt when the vampire sank her fangs into the fey's neck.

I frantically start scrubbing at the blood with my fingers as tears burn in my eyes. Is it my blood or the fey's? It doesn't really matter.

For a few minutes, I was her. I felt her pain. I felt what it was like when the blood was spilled from her throat.

"You landed in some blood when you fell," Jax says, sliding into the driver's seat. He shuts the door and watches me with worry. "That's where the blood came from."

I don't respond, my fingers moving violently against my flesh, desperate to wash off the blood and the memories.

"Alana, stop." He captures my hand and draws my fingers away. "You're making your skin bleed."

I glance at my reflection in the mirror and note the fresh wounds my fingernails inflicted along the base of my throat. Swallowing hard, I close the visor, highly aware his eyes are tracking every single one of my movements.

"You said you didn't faint," he says, letting go of my hand. "If that's not what happened, then what did?"

"I don't know," I mutter, flopping back in the seat.

"Okay . . . Then how do you know you didn't faint?"

"Because . . ." God, how can I even try to explain this to him? And should I even try to explain it to him?

His gaze bores into me. "Whatever it is, you can tell me."

"You don't know that for sure." I rest my head back against the seat and stare up at the ceiling. "Not when you have no idea what I'm about to say."

Silence drifts between us, and I shut my eyes. But the moment my eyelids close, red floods my vision, and I open them right back up.

"You know it took me a year to tell my parents I'd been bitten by a werewolf," he utters quietly. "And the only reason I told them was because they started questioning why I was disappearing all the time. And not just all the time, but whenever there was a full moon. The thing is that I probably could've told them right from the beginning, and their reaction would've been the same, but instead, I chose to suffer in silence for a year."

I turn my head toward him, and my gaze collides with his. "Did you feel better when you told them? I mean, were they understanding?"

"My mom was more understanding than my father." He rotates in the seat. "But even though my father . . . struggled with my change, I was still glad I told them because they were there to help me through it whenever I was struggling. My mom helped me more than my dad, but still . . . Without her, I don't know who I'd be today."

My thoughts drift back to Dash and the tension he carried when he spoke of their father. Jax's expression conveys the same stiffness at the mention of their dad, which makes me question just what kind of a man he is.

"How do you know I have a secret to tell?" I ask. "Maybe I'm just acting weird because the rotten stench of death plaguing the air is making me delirious."

"Werewolves have a sixth sense about these things." He extends his arm toward my neck and presses two fingers against my racing pulse. "Your pulse has been beating like crazy ever since you woke up. Something's wrong." His fingers trail down the side of my neck, sending shivers through my body. "You're scared for some reason."

Without removing my gaze from him, I point out at the field where the dead bodies lie. "Obviously."

"But you weren't scared when you first saw the scene. Not like this, anyway." He inhales deeply, and I cringe, wondering what he could possibly smell. "You're terrified. I can smell it."

He's right. I am terrified, a feeling I've only experienced a handful of times.

"FYI, that smelling thing you just did is super creepy," I joke, but my tone misses the mark. I shift in the seat, and his fingers fall away from my neck. "But you're right. Something did happen to me out on the field. Something bad. Something terrifying." A chill slithers up my spine as the fey's memories slink into my thoughts. "I think I might know who killed the fey."

He startles back, confusion swirling in his eyes. *"What?"*

"I saw something . . . when I touched one of the fey's arms . . ."

"Like a mark?"

"No . . ." I hesitate, knowing I'm going to sound crazy. But I have to tell him, have to convince him that what I saw is true so we can track down those vampires who slaughtered the fey and arrest them. Although I would way rather go the Keeper route on this and inflict the same pain on them as they did to the fey, that's not the Guardian way.

Le sigh.

"I'm not sure what you're trying to say," he says, totally lost.

I sigh. "I guess there's no easy way to say this, but when I touched the Fey's arm, I saw her thoughts. No, not just saw them, I lived them. And they weren't just any thoughts. They were the ones she had right before she died."

It takes a second for it to click, and then his eyes widen. "Wait a second. Are you saying that you saw who killed them?"

I nod, hoping upon hope that what happened to me is some sort of freaky Guardian trait I haven't learned about yet. "Yeah, I saw the whole thing play out through her eyes." I shake my head. "No, it was more than that. It was like I *was* her for a few minutes."

His mouth thins to a line as he presses his lips together. "Wait here. I need to go talk to Hadlee." He moves to get out of the car.

"Wait." I snag hold of the hem of his shirt and pull him to a stop. "What happened to me is normal, right? It happens to Guardians?"

"I'm sorry," he says with grave remorse. "I wish I could tell you that was it, but I've never heard of anything like this before."

My knuckles graze his back as I tighten my grasp on his shirt. "Then I don't want you telling Hadlee. I don't want anyone knowing about this, not until I know what's going on with me."

"I'm not going to tell Hadlee about that." He gives a stressing glance toward the front of the car where a group of five or six Guardians are standing around, talking and discussing the case. "I'm going to tell her that we're leaving, that you're sick, and I need to take you to the doctor."

"But you're not really taking me to the doctor, right?" I ask, releasing his shirt from my death grip.

"No, I'm taking you someplace safe where no one can overhear what we discuss, because if what you're saying is true . . . if you saw. . . ." He rubs his hand across his face so roughly his fingertips leave red marks on his skin. Then he gives a panicked glance at the people outside and leans in and lowers his voice. "If you saw what happened—saw the killer—and the wrong person finds out about it . . ." He doesn't finish.

He doesn't have to. I know.

If the wrong person finds out, I'll probably end up dead in a field just like the fey.

CHAPTER NINE

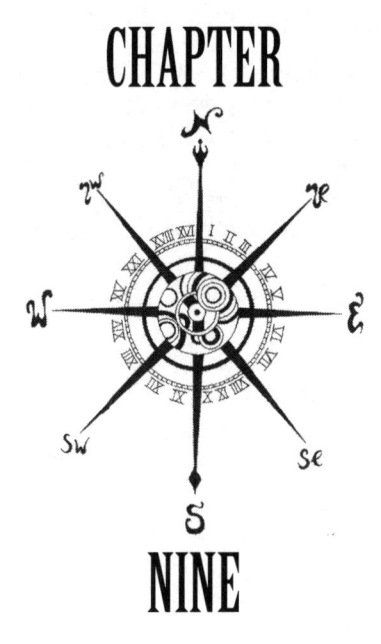

AFTER JAX LEAVES THE CAR to go tell Hadlee we're leaving, I crack the window, slump back in the seat, and try to sort through what just happened. While I don't know everything about the magical world, I've never heard of anyone being able to live other people's memories. Reading minds, sure. There's a spell that can do that. But actually living the memory, feeling what the person felt . . .

I shudder, reliving the awfulness. God, I hope that doesn't happen often.

This is only the start, Alana . . . my grandpa's voice appears again. *The start of your gifts . . . the start of your curse . . .*

"Curse?" I ask aloud. "What curse?"

Silence is my only answer.

I audibly sigh. "Where are you? And where do you go when

you grow quiet like that?"

Nothing.

I sigh again and rest my forehead against the cool glass. So I'm cursed with a gift, but what gift? And if this is only the start, does it mean I'm not only just a Guardian? What lies ahead for me?

Maybe I can ask my parents.

No!

The word screams in my head, but I'm unsure if the thought was mine or my grandpa's.

I get the message loud and clear, though, feel the severity all the way to my bones. Whatever is happening to me, it isn't a burden I need to put on my parents, at least until I find out more.

By the time Jax climbs into the car, I'm sweaty, exhausted, and confused. Jax looks stressed out, too, his hair sticking up as if he raked his fingers through the strands at least a hundred times.

"Ready?" he asks, slamming the door and turning the key in the ignition.

The engine rumbles to life, and he shoves the shifter into reverse and backs out onto the road.

I straighten in the seat and draw my seatbelt over my shoulder. "I think I'd be more ready if you told me where we are going."

"To see a friend of mine." Once the car is on the road, he pushes the shifter into drive and moves forward in the opposite direction of the academy.

I refuse to look at the field as we pass by it, afraid of what I might feel.

"A friend who doesn't live at the academy, I'm guessing."

"Nope. He lives a few towns over." He steers the car around a Jeep partially blocking the road then presses on the gas and peels out, leaving the bloody massacre in our tracks. "I don't want to take you back to the academy just yet, not until we find out more about what's going on with you."

"And how do you plan on doing that? Because I have no clue what happened to me."

"Me, either, but this friend of mine knows way more than I do."

"Why? What is he?"

His knuckles turn white as his grip on the wheel tightens. "I'd rather not tell you until I get there."

"Well, now you have to tell me or else I won't go."

"And how do you plan on doing that? By jumping out of the moving car?"

I shrug. "It wouldn't be the first time."

He heaves a frustrated sigh. "Fine, I'll tell you, but you can't freak out." He pauses, deliberating, and his frustration morphs into curiosity. "Have you really jumped out of a moving car before?"

I hold up three fingers. "Three times, and I have a wicked scar on my thigh to prove it." I lower my hand to my lap. "But don't change the subject. Tell me what this guy we're going to see is."

He taps his fingers against the top of the steering wheel, restless and uneasy. "He's an Enchanter."

My fingers instantly seek the door handle as I seriously consider bailing, just jumping out of the car while it's moving seventy miles an hour and letting the asphalt tear me apart.

"Alana," he warns. "Stop thinking like a Keeper. Just because Oliver is an Enchanter, it doesn't make him a bad person."

"Yeah, but it does make him a person who can possess people's minds." I withdraw my hand from the door, but the idea of jumping out still sounds more appealing than lounging around with some dude who can turn me into his own personal puppet. Sure, their sorcerer blood makes them a walking magical dictionary, but I don't know if I'm that desperate yet. "I've heard stories about Enchanters, terrible stories where they make people do horrible things."

"And there are some Enchanters who will use their power for that kind of purpose, but I've known Oliver since we were kids, and he's a good guy." He removes a hand from the wheel and places it on my leg, right above my kneecap. "I need you to trust me on this, okay?"

I stare down at his hand. "Is the touching thing some sort of wolf persuasion tactic?"

"Maybe." His lips quirk. "Is it working?"

I start to shake my head and lie, but then sigh. "Fine. I won't judge Oliver until I meet him."

"Good. I'm glad you see it my way." He gently squeezes my knee.

I bite down on my tongue. "Fine. I'll let you win this one."

Instead of grinning, he frowns. "Are you sure you didn't hit your head?"

"Ha, ha, you're such a riot." I slump back in the seat. "I'm just tired, okay? It's been a long morning."

"Just promise me you'll tell me if you start feeling strange." Worry laces his tone. "We have no idea what happened to you, so we don't know if there are going to be any side effects."

I nod, agreeing that I will. Then we settle into small chitchat as we drive down miles of desolate highway and pass through quaint, little towns.

I want to talk about what happened, try to figure out more before we get to this Enchanter dude, but I have the impression Jax is purposefully avoiding the subject. I don't know why other than perhaps he thinks we're still at risk of someone eavesdropping on our conversation.

We're just veering toward the outskirts of another town when my phone rings. I fish it out of my pocket, and my mood goes up a notch when I see the call is from Jayse, my cousin and best friend.

"Hey," I answer. "I'm glad you called. I could really use Jayse-cheer-me-up time."

"I must have read your mind." Nervousness rings in his tone. "Look, Alana, I really wish I could say I called just to say hello, but this isn't a friendly phone call."

"Okay." I stiffen, recalling the incident with the Transition Re-programmer. "What's going on? You're not in any trouble, are you? Because you're only allowed to get into trouble when you're with me."

"No . . . well, not really, I guess." He doesn't sound too convincing. "It's actually you I'm worried about."

"Me? I'm fine," I lie. "It's you I'm more worried about. I mean, we still haven't talked about that thing . . ." I leave the silent statement out there.

I never told Jayse that I know he's been using a Transition Re-programmer and that I know he's transitioning into something. He knows I think he's keeping something from me, and he told me he'd tell me when he's ready. Part of me hopes he's ready to talk now, because I really want to understand what he's going through, why he has been acting so distant lately. Another part of me hopes maybe he'll wait until I'm a little more stable.

"I promise this has nothing to do with me," he says. "It has to do with the territory clan of vampires."

My thoughts float back to the fey's memory . . .

A tattoo of a blood droplet with a silvery T is carved into the center. She's part of the territory clan . . .

I flinch, coming out of the memory, hyperaware Jax is observing me instead of the road.

"Okay, what's going on with them? And why are you telling me?"

"Because . . ." His nerves show through his uneven tone. "There's a rumor going around that they killed a bunch of fey near the academy."

"That may or may not be true," I say, uncertain if I'm allowed to talk to him about the case.

"I'm guessing you can't tell me, but that's okay. I didn't call for clarification. I called to warn you that there's a rumor going around that, a while ago, the entire clan was captured by some group that runs tests on paranormal creatures." He pauses, as if waiting for me to say something, but I'm not about to utter a damn word about the Electi and put him at risk. "I'm not sure what happened to the vampires during these test, but I guess they were released and sent to eliminate as much of the North Kingdom Fey as they could. From what I understand, they somehow set them up to meet them in some field near the academy then killed a bunch of them."

I swallow hard. "You might be right, but I'm not sure why you're telling me this."

He remains silent for a beat or two. "Because there's also another rumor going around that part of the reason the fey were slaughtered was because they were testing something out. I'm not sure what, but I know you're living close to the area, and you could be working the case . . . and I'm just . . ." He releases a loud breath. "I'm just worried about you. I know how much you love to be in the middle of battle, but I really think you should keep a safe distance from this one."

"Battle?" I sit up straight as he catches my undivided attention. "What battle?"

"The battle the North Kingdom Fey just declared on the Territory Vampire Clan," he says in an ominous tone. "I guess the fey who survived are pissed off and want their revenge."

My fingers fold inward, stabbing into my palms as images of the murders plague my thoughts. "I don't really blame them. What happened . . . It was sickening . . ."

"Alana, promise me you won't get involved with this."

Concern floods his tone. "Some serious shit is about to go down between fey and vampire, and you know how powerful they both are. Plus, I've heard that the princess of the North Kingdom is trying to persuade the water fey to join her side. I guess she was spotted last night somewhere, having some secret chat with the empress of the water fey."

A wave of suspicion builds inside me. "Where did this happen exactly?"

"I'm not sure, and it doesn't really matter." The unexpected harshness in his voice startles me. "I just wanted to give you a heads up that a lot of bad stuff might start happening, and while I know you want to help, I want you to stay out of this."

I want to confess everything to him, explain to him that I can't stay out of it. I'm neck deep in it. But then I'd have to explain why, and I don't want to bring him into my mess.

"I'll try my best," I lie, my chest squeezing with guilt.

When we were kids, Jayse and I used to tell each other almost everything. Lately, though, it feels like a sea of lies is between us.

"You're okay, though, right? Not just with this whole battle going on, but just with . . . life, I guess?"

"Yeah, everything's fine. Everything's great," he lies through his teeth. "Look, I have to go. Just be careful, okay?"

"You, too," I say softly. "And call me if you ever want to talk."

"I will soon. I promise." He sounds like he's being truthful this time, yet it pains him to do it. I have to wonder why. What's so bad that he doesn't want to tell me?

What has he turned into?

CHAPTER TEN

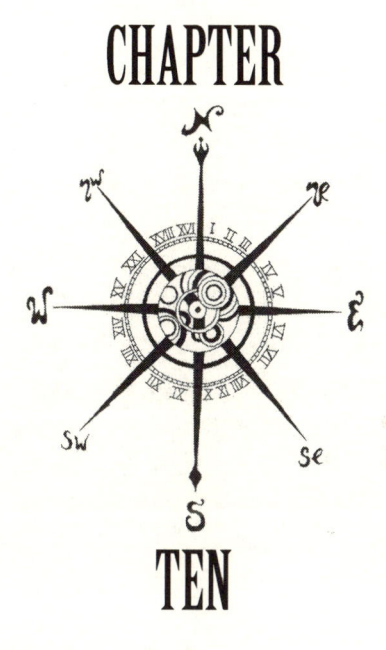

AFTER I HANG UP, I aim a finger at Jax. "All right, I'm going to ask you a question, and you have to promise you'll be completely honest."

"I can't make that promise without knowing what the question is." He puts on his sunglasses and concentrates on the road. "But you can ask, and we'll see where it goes."

Frowning, I lower my finger. "Is Vivianne fey?"

He turns, appearing taken aback. "Why would you ask that?"

"Because Jayse just told me that the princess of the North Kingdom and the empress of the water fey had a secret rendezvous last night."

"What?"

"Yeah, he didn't say where, but I guess the meeting was

about seeking revenge on . . ." Wait. I haven't told him about the vampire clan yet, and he doesn't want me to until we get to the Enchanter's place. "Seeking revenge for the fey who died last night."

"So the fey know who killed their own?"

"According to Jayse, they do. I'm sure he got the information from the Keepers, so he's probably right."

"Not necessarily." He drums his fingers against the top of the shifter. "I've never noticed the fey mark on Vivianne before, but that doesn't mean it doesn't exist. She could be both fey and Guardian, keeping her fey blood hidden for whatever reason. I know a few people who keep their bloodline hidden pretty well, but it'd be highly unlikely for her to keep royal fey blood a secret."

"But not impossible," I say. "And if she's just a princess, as of now, that means she's not reigning yet. And I've heard of fey royalty keeping their identities a secret to protect themselves."

"But who would Vivianne be protecting herself from?"

"I don't know, but honestly, I wouldn't be surprised if she had enemies lining up to take her down. The woman's a bitch."

He keeps restlessly thrumming his fingers against the shifter over and over again until the sound starts to drive me mad.

"God, what if she is?" he mumbles after a minute of tapping goes by. "What if she's been the princess this entire time and has been hiding it from everyone?"

I tuck a strand of hair behind my ear. "Then she's pretty good at hiding stuff, which makes me wonder what else she's hiding."

"Yeah, me, too." He ceases the tapping and brings his hand to the wheel. "I think, when we get to Oliver's place, I'm going to call Dash and have him check out the forest to make sure Vivianne and the empress weren't just having a friendly meeting out there."

"I think that's a good idea." I sink back in the seat and stare out the window, reflecting over everything we just discussed.

If it turns out Vivianne is fey and is the princess of the North Kingdom, then it makes me wonder if maybe there's a bigger reason for her wanting to find the Dagger of Conspectu than just finding it and returning it to the vault.

I make a mental note that, when we get to a safe-to-speak-freely zone, I'll ask Jax if he knows what the dagger does and cross my fingers that my hiding place for the mysterious weapon remains a secret.

CHAPTER ELEVEN

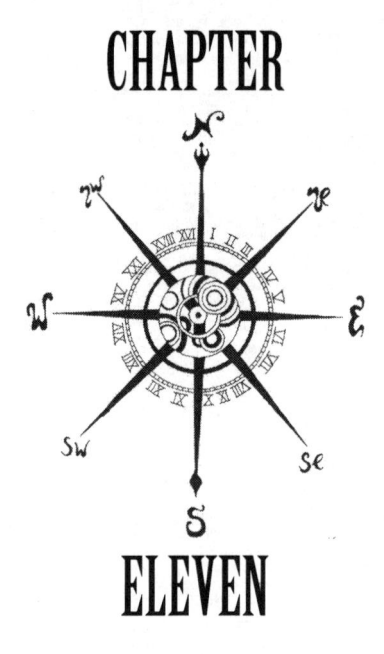

"SO, THIS IS WHAT AN Enchanter's house looks like," I say as I stand in front of a quaint-looking wooden cottage located at the end of a dirt road about two miles out of the center of town.

"What were you expecting?" Jax moves up beside me and lifts his fist to knock on the door.

"I don't know." I shrug, glancing at the bright red tulips growing all along the cottage. "A dungeon in a castle."

He shoots me a warning look. "Remember what you promised."

"I know. I won't judge him until I meet him." I stuff my hands into my back pockets. "I'm sorry I said that. I guess old habits die hard."

"Well, they should completely die right now." He knocks on

the wooden door again. "Don't bring your judgment inside here, okay? Ollie's had a rough life as it is."

I want to ask him what's been rough about his life, but the door swings open before I get a chance.

I measure up the guy standing in the doorway with extreme curiosity. He is definitely younger than I was expecting, around the same age as Jax, which I guess is logical since he said they were friends when they were kids. He has an edgy, gothic look going on, dressed head to toe in black with an array of studded leather bracelets matching the belt looping through his jeans. His skin is as pale as a vampire, his chin-length black hair hangs in his eyes, metal studs run all along one brow, and gauges ornament his ears. His sullen expression fits in well with his grungy attire. That is, until he grins.

"Jax?" He sticks out his hand for a fist bump. "It's been a long time. Too long if you ask me."

"Yes, it has." Jax taps his fist against Oliver's with an easy smile on his face, something I'm pretty certain I haven't witnessed before. "What has it been, like a year?"

"I think the last time we hung out was last Christmas." He's all smiles until he glances at me. Then his happiness changes to intrigue as he sizes me up. "So, who's the girl?"

"Oh, this is Alana." Jax gestures at me. "Alana's from the academy. She's a first year, and I'm stuck training her."

"Stuck, huh?" He bites his lip, finding this funny for some reason.

"Ollie, don't start," Jax warns, drawing his sunglasses to the top of his head.

Oliver raises his hands in surrender, but a hint of amusement glimmers in his eyes. "All right, I won't. But I just want to point out that only you would look at spending time with a beautiful girl as a negative thing."

"Don't let her beauty fool you." Jax casts me a sidelong

glance. "She's a pain in the ass when she opens her mouth."

"Hey." I lightly shove him, and he stumbles to the side, almost falling off the front porch. "Like you're any better."

He effortlessly regains his balance, and a grin spans across his face as he looks at Ollie. "See what I mean?"

I shoot him a dirty look. "You're just as much a pain in the ass as I am." I put my hands on my hips. "You're always so hot and cold all the time. Ever since I met you, I've been dealing with emotional whiplash."

Jax continues to grin. "Like you're any better."

"Hey, I'm not moody," I insist. "If anything, I'm happy all the time."

He gives an exaggerated eye roll. "Yeah, you sure seemed happy when I met you. If I remember right, I think you called me a brooding, cocky asshole."

"You are a brooding, cocky asshole," I retort. "And that was mild in comparison to you threatening to kill me."

He steps toward me. "Well, you would've gotten yourself killed if I hadn't."

"I was never going to try and kill that vampire." I inch forward until the tips of my clunky boots clip his. "I'd already bailed out on my plan before you came along."

He laughs, shaking his head. "Bullshit. You were still thinking about it."

"Maybe," I say truthfully. "But I didn't. You did."

His tone drops, his low tone containing a warning. "I already told you it wasn't me."

"I know you did," I say, blowing out a sigh. "Why are we even talking about this? It's not even important right now."

"I think he might just like to get you all worked up," Oliver states, watching us with amusement. "In fact, I think he enjoys it a lot."

Jax's gaze darts to Oliver, his silver eyes shooting daggers.

Oliver simply laughs and sticks out a hand toward me. "I'm Oliver, by the way. Or Ollie, anyway. No one calls me Oliver except my parents."

I take his hand and shake it. "It's nice to meet you in person. When Jax said he had a friend, I honestly didn't believe him at first. But here you are, living proof that Jax can actually make friends."

"Alana," Jax starts at the same time Ollie lets out a snort.

"I like her," he declares to Jax, releasing my hand.

"I figured you would," Jax mumbles then sighs heavily. "Look, I'd love to say I came here to hang out, but there's some really important stuff I need to talk to you about."

"I kind of figured that," Ollie replies, his humor fading.

Jax's brows draw together. "And why's that?"

Ollie sweeps the flowery field and leafy trees enclosing his cottage with his gaze then steps aside and motions us to come in. "Come on in. We shouldn't talk out here. Who knows who could be listening."

Jax steps over the threshold without hesitating, and I do the same. Jax was right about holding off judgment of Ollie until I met him. I'm not getting a creepy, I'm-going-to-turn-you-into-my-puppet vibe from him. In fact, he seems like a really nice guy, and the inside of his house is wicked cool.

Not only does the living room have a mural of The Forest of Shadows and Bones, a ghostly forest located in Scotland, painted on the wall, but weapons are everywhere.

"Oh, my God, you have a Vanishing Blade," I say excitedly as I spot a glinting silver sword mounted on his living room wall, along with a ton of other knives, daggers, and swords. "That's so awesome."

"It's pretty cool." He closes the front door and steps up beside me. "It'd be cooler if I actually could use them, but I've never been that great at using weapons. I'm more of a magic, spell, enchantment kind of guy."

"Maybe I could teach you," I offer. "I'm not fantastic or anything, but I'm not bad, either. And I had great teachers."

Ollie offers me a strange look, and Jax intervenes.

"Alana's parents are Keepers." He moves to the other side of me, standing so close our arms brush.

"Really?" Ollie examines me with fascination. "You know, I've never met a Keeper before."

I try not to frown at the reminder that I'm not a Keeper. The disappointment isn't nearly as bad as when I first found out, though.

"Well, I'm not really a Keeper. I've just been trained by them and not fully trained, either."

"It's still pretty cool." A thoughtful look crosses his face. "Maybe I'll take you up on your offer to teach me."

When I feel Jax stiffen beside me, I toss a glance over my shoulder.

"What's the matter with you?" I mouth. He's the one who told me I could trust Ollie.

The irritation in his eyes dwindles and is masked by coolness as he shrugs.

I shake my head. *What a weirdo.*

I return my attention to Ollie. "You know what, I'd love to teach you sometime."

He smiles at that before his gaze travels to Jax. Then Ollie smashes his lips together.

"Okay, then," Ollie says to no one in particular.

"Should we sit down and talk about some stuff?" Jax asks, sounding a bit peeved.

"Sure." Ollie's smile returns, bright and shiny like a glittery rainbow. "You guys sit down. I'm going to grab a couple of things." He strides across the living room toward an arched doorway.

"Your house is still under the praesidium spell, right?" Jax shouts out after him.

Ollie pauses in the doorway and glances at Jax with uneasiness. "Yeah, and there's praesidium all around the house, too, so you're good to say whatever you need to." His uneasiness vanishes. "Does anyone want a soda or something?"

"I'll have a glass of water," Jax says, plopping down onto a leather sofa.

"A soda sounds good to me," I tell him with a gracious smile.

He smiles back at me before ducking through the doorway and stepping into the kitchen.

I join Jax on the sofa, keeping a marginal distance. "So, what's up with you not wanting me to teach Ollie?"

He picks at a crack in the cushion. "I never said that."

"You didn't have to," I tell him, resting my arm on the armrest. "Your brooding silence said it for you."

He shifts his silvery eyes to me. "I just think that you two spending time together like that isn't a good idea."

"Why not?"

"Because I said so."

"That's not a very good reason," I tell him. "In fact, it might be the worst reason ever."

"Nah, I've heard worse." He relaxes back and stretches his arm across the back of the sofa. "So, are you going to tell me what you saw?"

"You mean in the fey woman's memories?" I ask, getting whiplash from the subject change.

He nods, his fingers brushing strands of my hair. "I want you to tell me as much as you can. Don't push yourself or anything, though. I know it was hard on you when it happened."

"But what did happen?" I ask aloud while internally wondering why the heck he's touching my hair. "You said Ollie might be able to help us figure that out, but how?"

"I'll explain when he gets back here." Another comb of his fingers through my hair. What the bejesus is he doing? "But let's start at the beginning when you first started seeing the fey's memories. Or did it start before that?"

"It might have been before that." I take a deep breath and prepare myself to relive the horror that happened on the field.

CHAPTER TWELVE

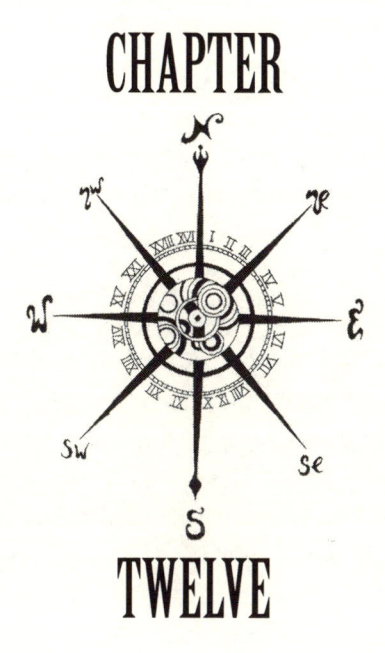

I BEGIN WITH THE STRANGE feeling I experienced in front of the school and keep going all the way until the part where the vampire was about to attack Adaliya. After that, I struggle, on the verge of tears as the fear and horror she felt when she died rise up inside me.

Jax remains quiet the entire time, and a tiny part of me worries he might think I'm insane.

"So, what do you think?" I ask after I've finished explaining everything.

"You want to know what I think?" Jax asks, but it's more of a rhetorical question. He slants forward on the sofa and rests his head in his hands, massaging his scalp, making his light blond hair go all bedhead crazy. "I think we have a huge problem on our hands."

"Because there's about to be a huge battle between the fey and the vampires?"

"No . . . Well, that's part of it. But I'm honestly not too concerned about that."

"How can you not be concerned about that?" I ask with a dumbfounded shake of my head. "A battle is about to break out between two very powerful groups, and they could end up destroying the entire world."

He raises his head and looks at me. "The battle's not going to break out, because we're going to do our job and make the proper arrests. The territory clan will be tried for their crimes, and then the fey will no longer have a reason to start the battle."

"You plan on tracking down and arresting an entire clan of vampires? A clan of vampires who came from experimental facilities?" I shake my head. "Jax, Jax, Jax, how have you survived for the last nineteen years?"

"I think you're forgetting one important thing about me." His eyes illuminate, glowing silver. "I'm not just a Guardian, Alana." The glow in his eyes fades. "And vampires fear wolves."

Okay, he has me there.

"All right, I'm sorry I doubted your capability," I apologize, and his lips twitch with an impending smile. "So, we're really doing this? We're really going after the territory clan?" Hope sparkles inside me like a shiny new Foreseer ball. Do I really get to hunt the killers down?

"*We're* not doing anything," he stresses, dimming my hope into a tiny lightning bug. "*I'm* going after them."

"Hey, I'm capable enough to at least help a little."

"Capable, yes. But with what's going on with you . . ." His Adam's apple bobs as he swallows hard. "I don't think it's a good idea for you to put yourself in danger, not until we can figure out what's going on with you."

"I might be able to help with that." Ollie appears in the

doorway, carrying a glass of water and two cans of Coke. "I'm sorry I was listening, but I walked in mid-conversation, and with how upset she was . . ." He walks farther into the room, glancing from me to Jax. "I figured it might be better if I listened so she didn't have to repeat it."

"It's fine." Jax reaches to take the glass of water from his hand. "So, you know what's going on with her?"

"That all depends"—he hands me a can of soda—"on if she has the mark of a Necromancer."

"That's what you think's going on with me?" Goose bumps sprout across my arms. "You think I can talk to and raise the dead?"

"That's just a theory." He takes a seat in the recliner across from the sofa and sets his soda on coffee table. "But, if you don't have the mark, then it's probably something else."

"Like what?" I wonder. "What other things can communicate and see the thoughts of the dead?"

He shrugs. "I have no idea, but there are ways to find out."

I tap the top of the can with my finger, pop the tab, and the soda inside bubbles. "What kind of ways?"

"I don't think that's a good idea," Jax cuts in, setting his glass of water down on the coffee table.

"It was just a suggestion." Ollie opens his soda, sits back on the recliner, and takes a sip. "But it would be a hell of a lot easier than going door to door, asking every Enchanter out there if they've heard of anything like this before."

"Wait, he's not talking about the Scrawl of Secrets, is he?" My gaze bounces back and forth between them. "But that seems a little risky, considering it's locked up in Hushing Forest, which FYI, only pixies know where that is. Plus, it's dangerous, so dangerous the Keepers won't even step foot in there."

"No one said you were going." Jax brushes me off with his eyes on Ollie. "You think it might have answers?"

"It's probably your best bet." Ollie props his foot on his knee and takes a swig of his soda. "And it's probably less dangerous than talking to Enchanters. Cross paths with one who's not as nice as me, and you'll end up under their enchantment until you die."

Jax cracks his knuckles against the sides of his legs. "You think you could find a pixie that you could make lead us there?"

The way he says "make" has me speculating if Ollie is going to enchant this pixie into taking Jax. I'd feel bad for the pixie, but I really want to find out what's going on with me.

"I'm sure I can, but it might take a couple of weeks to get close to one. Pixies have a keen sense of when an Enchanter is close by, and they tend to stay away from us. I don't really blame them, though." He smiles at me, but it looks all sorts of wrong, filled with self-hate and torture. "What we can do *is* rather terrifying. I'd probably stay clear of me, too."

I feel sorry for him and awful for how I reacted when I first heard he was an Enchanter. He's obviously experienced a lot of anguish because of what he is.

I really need to stop jumping to conclusions before I meet people.

The thought is very un-Keeper like and makes me wonder if perhaps I'm starting to change from the girl who flipped out when her Guardian mark appeared. That need to eliminate first and ask questions later is gradually diminishing. Maybe one day, I won't react when Jax mentions a vampire, fey, Enchanter, ogre, or any other paranormal creature.

"But you think you can do it?" I ask Ollie. "And you'd be willing to do it?"

He nods, sweeping strands of hair out of his eyes. "I'd be happy to. It'll make me feel useful for once."

Before Jax or I can say anything, he scoots to the edge of the seat and places the can back on the table.

"Do you mind if I check something first before I set out on

this pixie tracking mission?"

"Sure." I take a long gulp of soda.

"I promise it won't hurt," he adds, rising to his feet. "But I'm really curious if you have any traces of fey magic in you."

I choke on my soda. "Holy shit." I cough. "You can do that?"

He nods, kneeling down on the hardwood floor in front of me. "I just need you to let me relax you for a second."

I glance at Jax, and he nods with assurance. Setting the soda down, I inch to the edge of the seat and rest my hands in my lap.

"All right, you can do it."

He gives a seemingly genuine smile, but he swiftly composes himself, reaches for my face, and cups a hand around each side of my head. Looking straight into my eyes, his lips begin to move as he chants what sounds like gibberish underneath his breath. His pupils begin to swirl, vivid shades of blue sparkling against the sunlight.

"So pretty . . ." I hear myself murmur.

Ollie's lips quirk, but he bites back the smile and continues gazing into my eyes, drawing me in to his hypnotic gaze. My muscles relax until my body feels as weightless as clouds. It makes me want to fly. And sing. And dance. Do anything and everything.

"Blink for me, Alana," Ollie whispers softly. "And the enchantment will wear off."

My head bobs from side to side. "No way . . . This feels too nice."

Ollie presses his lips together, stifling a laugh, and I hear Jax sigh.

"Alana." Jax's scent kisses my senses. "You need to blink."

"You smell good," I murmur. "Like trees . . . and yumminess."

Ollie rubs his hand across his mouth, struggling not to laugh. "She's a stubborn one."

"Yes, she is," Jax agrees. He says something in a low tone that makes Ollie move back. Then he shifts in front of me. "Blink, Alana," he demands.

His demanding tone shatters the high in my body, and my eyelids open and close.

"That was weird." I rub my eyes as reality sinks in. "I felt like I was drunk or something."

It all comes crashing back to me. Oh, my God, did I tell Jax he smelled yummy! Great. It's only a matter of time before he throws that in my face.

"Yeah," Jax agrees, as if he has experienced it before. He turns to Ollie, who's now sitting on the corner of the coffee table, studying me. "So, what's the verdict? Does she have traces of fey magic in her?"

"She doesn't just have traces of fey magic in her. It's entangled in her like a web." He scratches his head. "And the quantities are almost as much as a faerie would have."

My heart constricts inside my chest as I stare down at the light bluish purple blood veins barely visible in my forearms. "But I don't have faerie blood in me."

"I know you don't," Ollie tells me. "That much, I can tell."

"So what does this mean?" I ask. "Will the magic fade eventually?"

"Probably," Ollie says. "But I'm guessing, until it does, there might be some side effects."

I swallow hard. "Like what?"

"I'm not one hundred percent sure." He tugs his fingers through his hair. "But usually, if someone temporarily steals magic from a faerie, their emotions connect for a while."

I frown. "Great, so I'm going to end up feeling what a dead faerie feels."

"I'm not positive since I'm not sure what's going on with you. I just wanted to give you a warning in case you start feeling strange." Ollie stands to his feet and wanders toward the kitchen again.

"Where are you going?" Jax calls after him.

Ollie glances over his shoulder at Jax. "To go track down a pixie so we can find out what she is before anyone else does."

He exits the room, leaving me alone with Jax and my over-analyzing thoughts of what could possibly be going on with me.

CHAPTER THIRTEEN

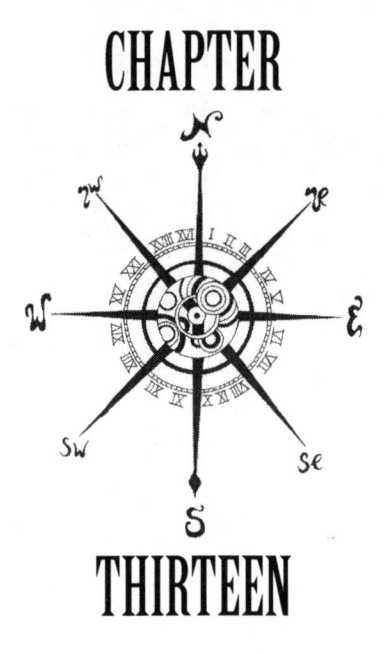

AN HOUR LATER, OLLIE SETS off on his pixie tracking quest with the promise that he'll get ahold of Jax the moment he finds out where Hushing Forest is. He leaves us alone in the cottage so Jax and I can discuss a few things in private and figure out our next move. I also take the chance to use the bathroom and wash the blood off my face and neck.

After splashing a few handfuls of cold water on my face, I pat my skin dry and assess the damage in the mirror.

"Jesus, I look like the undead." I slant forward over the sink and squint at the dark half-circles under my eyes, my pallid skin, and my tangled mess of brown hair.

I didn't look this bad this morning. Did what happened on the field take a small nick out of my health? Is the lingering magic inside me doing this? I shudder at the thought. I hope it doesn't happen again. And I hope the magic leaves my body. It's not like I have any use for faerie magic since I'm not fey, and I can't use it.

Or can I?

Stepping back from the mirror, I stare at my reflection and attempt to put up a glamour, make my hair change colors, make my skin shimmer, make my eyes glow.

Nope. Nothing.

I grip the edge of the sink. So, if I can't use the magic, then what's the point?

In time, Alana . . . You'll learn . . . how to . . . use . . . your . . . gift. My grandpa's voice is feeble inside my head. *I have to go for . . . a while . . . There's too much . . . magic around . . . right . . . now.*

A weighted exhale puffs from my lips. "There you go again with your cryptic messages and disappearing act. I wish you were just here. Then maybe I could have someone to talk to."

For some reason, I expect him to materialize. He doesn't.

Sighing, I comb my fingers through my hair and pull it into a side braid with an elastic that I find in one of the drawers. Then I return to living room where Jax is lounging on the sofa, fiddling with his phone.

"So, what do we do now?" I ask, plopping down on the sofa beside him. "What's the plan for finding these vampires?"

"*We* aren't doing anything." He punches a few buttons on his phone. "*I'm* going to track down some vampires and make some arrests. I need to get a confession from one of them, though, because we can't use what happened to you as evidence."

"I should be able to help you." I pick at the tab of my empty soda can. "This is Guardian business, and I'm a Guardian, too." I crunch my soda can up and drop it on the table. "Besides, I can identify the vampire who killed Adaliya." I crack my knuckles. "And, with the right amount of torture, I should be able to get a confession out of her along with a list of names of the other vampires who were there."

His gaze cuts to me with a frown on his lips. "No one's going to be torturing anyone. That's not how we do things."

"It might not be how we do things, but it's definitely an easy way to get the truth out of someone," I say. Since I really want to go with him, though, I tack on, "But if you don't want me to torture anyone, I won't."

His phone buzzes in his hand, but he doesn't glance at the screen. His eyes stay fastened on me, assessing me, while he contemplates what I said for a lengthy amount of time.

"First years aren't supposed to go on arrests," he says.

My lips part to entice him with more reasons he should take me, but he continues before I get an opportunity.

"However, you made a good point about being able to identify the vampire. This will go a lot more quickly if I have a single target to zero in on instead of spending days searching and asking around."

I resist the urge to get too excited just yet. "So, I get to go?"

He surrenders with a sigh. "Yeah, you get to go."

"Yes!" I fist pump the air. "Finally, some action work." God, I've missed it.

"But," he speaks loudly over my celebration, "you have to agree that you'll listen to everything I say. If I tell you to do something, you do it."

"Yes, sir," I say with a grin and a salute.

He rubs his scruffy jawline. "You know, I'm really starting to like this whole sir thing." His eyes suddenly glimmer mischievously, and his mouth opens to say something I'm pretty sure I won't like. "Probably about as much as you like how I smell."

And there we go. He lasted a whole hour.

"That was the enchantment talking," I lie breezily. "Honestly, I kind of think you smell—"

"Yummy." His goofy, arrogant grin makes me want to slap

him.

Well, sort of. Truthfully, he kind of looks adorable enough to kiss.

I blink the thought from my head. *Just stop, Alana. Don't go there.*

"Whatever." I decide to own up to the truth. "I think you smell yummy, but I also think cookies smell yummy, too."

Something about what I say makes his expression falter. It takes a second for me to figure out what might be wrong. Dash smells like cookies. Does he think I'm saying Dash smells yummy, too? Why would it matter? I mean, how can a guy who smells like cookies not smell yummy?

"We should probably get going." He checks the time on his phone. "The sun's about to go down, and then we have about eight hours to get this done before the vamps have to hole up underground and indoors again." He starts to get up, but I catch his arm, stopping him.

"There's one more thing I want to talk to you about while we're here and can speak freely." I let go of his sleeve and wait for him to sit back down before continuing. "The Dagger of Conspectu . . . What does it do exactly?"

A crease forms at his brows. "You don't know?"

I shake my head. "I think I've heard of it, but not enough to know what it does."

He rubs his hand across his forehead. "Well, legend has it that, if used right, it can steal the magical power out of any paranormal creature."

"I don't . . ." I breathe. "That's . . ."

"Dangerous?" he says for me, and I nod. "It's also next to impossible since no one's ever figured out how to use it."

I swallow hard, my heart an erratic mess. Jax's worried expression mirrors mine, probably because he's thinking the same thing.

If no one knows how to use the dagger, then why did my grandpa go through so much trouble to steal it from The Vault?

CHAPTER FOURTEEN

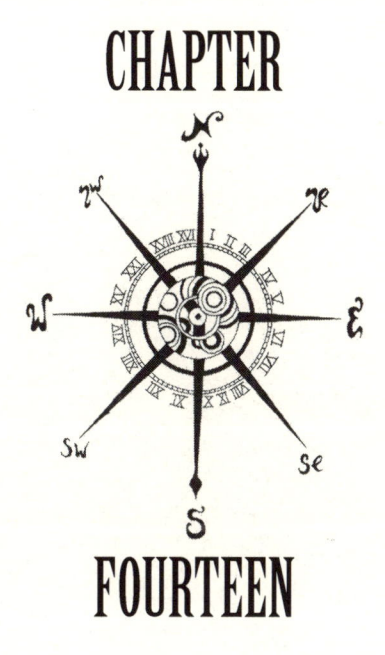

"WHERE ARE WE GOING EXACTLY?" I ask Jax after we hit the road. The sky is tinted a pale pink as the sun descends and the moon and stars rise. My window is down, and a cool breeze blows into the cab, airing out the smell of greasy burgers and fries coming from the fast food we picked up a few minutes ago. "I know that particular clan hangs out near Virginia Beach, but do you know some of the locations they hang out at?"

Nodding, Jax punches in an address in his phone's GPS. "But I need to make another stop before we get into that."

I dunk a fry into a cup of ranch and pop it into my mouth. "Where?"

He balances his phone on the dashboard. "To a friend of mine."

"You have another *friend*?" I say with mocking shock as I take out a burger from the brown paper bag.

A smile plays at the corners of his lips. "I do, actually. And this one is going to take a look at the photo that I took of the symbol." He reaches to take the burger as I offer it to him. "Plus, they're the person I was telling you about who can look at your phone, tell us who put the bug on it, and maybe help us debug it."

"That's good. I'm getting sick of lying to everyone who calls me." I dig out another burger from the bag, unwrap it, and take a huge bite, feeling famished.

"Who've you been lying to?" He opens his mouth and dives into his burger, eating half of it in nearly one bite.

"My mom called me this morning." I stir a fry around in the cup of ranch. "It's not like I plan on telling her everything—I won't risk her life like that. I've always been pretty honest with her, though, except for this morning. And I definitely didn't like it."

He picks a pickle off his burger and tosses it onto the wrapper spread across his lap. "It's good you can be honest with her—I mean, under normal circumstances."

I stuff a fry into my mouth and wipe my greasy fingers off on a napkin. "Are you close with your mom?"

He lifts a shoulder and shrugs. "Not really."

I toss the napkin into the paper bag. "But you said your mom helped you after you told her you'd been turned into a wolf."

"She did help me, but that doesn't mean we're close." He reaches for the fries on my lap and steals a handful. "I've never really been close with either of my parents."

"How come?" When he masks his expression, I add, "Never mind. You don't have to tell me if it's too personal." I slip off my shoes and get comfortable as I nibble on a ranch-drenched fry. "My mom and Jayse have always told me I have no filter when it comes to asking questions."

"They're right," he agrees with an exaggerated nod.

I chuck a fry at him, and it pegs him in the forehead. "Hey, you haven't known me long enough to state that with such confidence."

"I may not have known you for very long, but I knew from the first time you opened your mouth that you had no filter."

"Right back at ya, werewolf dude," I say with a wicked smile. "You're just as blunt as me."

His burger oozes ketchup down his hand, and he licks it off. "I guess it's a good thing we got paired up, then, huh?"

I take another bite of my burger. "I don't know about that. We butt heads *a lot*."

"Yeah, but we also work well together." He finishes off his burger then chases it with a swig of his chocolate shake.

I raise my brows at him with doubt. "We do?"

He shrugs, crumpling the burger wrapper and discarding it into the bag. "This is the quickest I've ever solved a case."

"Yeah, but I think that only happened because of my freaky tuning-into-a-dead-faerie's-mind thing," I say, reaching for my soda.

"That's not the only reason." He checks the GPS, flips on the blinker, and steers the car into the turning lane. "Although, I might retract my statement, depending on how tonight goes."

"I promise I'll be on my best behavior." I draw an X over my heart. "Cross my heart and hope to die."

He tosses a wolfish grin in my direction. "How about just cross your heart? I don't think you should be making any promises about dying when it comes to you being on your best behavior."

I chuck another fry at him; only, he opens his mouth this time and catches it. Then he licks his lips and flashes me his pearly whites.

I shake my head and roll my eyes. "Show off."

The lightness in his eyes dims as he turns into the parking lot of a two-story steel warehouse. He makes a half-loop around the building, parking in the back near a flight of stairs that leads to a rusted metal door.

"So, this is where your friend lives?" I ask, eyeballing the door.

"They're not really a friend, just someone I go to sometimes when I need a favor." He glances into the rearview mirror and tousles his fingers through his hair until they're sticking up perfectly chaotically.

I suppress a smile. "Is this not-really-a-friend of the female gender by chance?"

He leans back from the mirror, his forehead furrowing. "Yeah. Why?"

I conceal my mouth behind my hand to stop myself from laughing. "Because you just turned into Mr. Primpy. Honestly, I thought you only had one level—Mr. Cocky, I Look Fantastic All the Time—but clearly, you've got more layers than I originally thought."

He extends his arm toward me, his finger splaying across the back of my seat, right beside my head. "Again, you sound jealous."

"And again, you falsely accuse me of being jealous." I open the door to get out. "I know this is going to be hard to believe, but not everyone's in love with you, Jax."

His eyebrow arches up in infuriating confidence. "Who said you were in love with me? Being jealous wouldn't mean you were in love with me. It'd just mean you're attracted to me and maybe kind of like me, both of which, you do." Grinning, he reaches for my face to do God knows what. I don't wait to find out.

I shove open the door the rest of the way and just about fall out of the car. I manage to catch myself before I eat dust and get my feet planted underneath me. I spin around and bump the door shut, smothering the sound of Jax's chuckling.

Moments later, he climbs out of the car with a confident smile on his face. "Ready to go in? Or do you want to fall out of the car again?"

"I didn't fall out." I round the car and walk past him, heading for the stairway. "I *almost* fell out. And that only happened because I was trying to get away from whatever you were about to do."

He strides after me, walking so closely his breath dusts my ear when he speaks. "You were flustered. Admit it." Our boots thud against the metal steps as we stomp up the stairs. "You were flustered because, deep down, you like me. You just don't want to admit it."

Almost to the top of the stairway, I reel on him. He's standing closer than I calculated, and I just about smack into him. He grips the railing, startled, but refuses to put space between us.

I cross my arms over my chest. "Is this your way of paying me back for the Truth Serum incident? Because I think we're getting pretty close to being even."

"We're not even close to being even." He slants toward me, his voice dropping an octave. "Do you have any idea how bad it is to be forced to say things against your will?"

"I've had a few possession spells cast on me before, so I actually do." I hold on to the railing as my heart thunders in my chest, either from the intensity of this conversation or his nearness—I'm not quite sure. "Look, Jax, I am sorry about what happened. I just felt like I had to, you know, or else I'd never get answers. But if I could go back, I'd probably have found a better way to get the truth out of you."

He rubs his lips together, considering something. "All right, I accept your apology, and I'll stop with the jealousy thing." I start to relax, but then he throws out a, "But I still need to pay you back so we're even."

I sigh. "Fine. Pay me back. Make us even. Then maybe we can move on from this."

"I'm glad I have your permission to get you back." He grins then pushes past me and climbs the rest of the stairs.

I follow after him, wondering how on earth he'll even things out between us. He warned me before that it wouldn't be magical. What will it be?

"You won't figure it out," he says when I reach his side.

I throw a cheeky grin at him. "Maybe not, but that doesn't mean I'm not going to try."

Chuckling, he raps his knuckles against the door. "You'll know when I do it because you'll feel as stupid as I did when I realized—"

The metal door swings open, and a faint mist laces the air as a woman in her early twenties appears in the doorway. "Jax, darling, how are you?" she purrs.

The first thought I have is, *no wonder Jax was fussing with his hair*, because the woman standing in front of me is absolutely stunning with long, auburn hair that flows in curls to the base of her back. Her lips are stained a fierce red that brings out the intense gold-green in her eyes. And her body is freaking amazing. The tight red dress she's wearing shows off her curvy and voluptuous frame. It makes me suddenly loathe my tall, lean, beanpole body. I seriously just want to . . .

Wait a second . . .

My gaze drops to her legs and scrolls up all the way to her neck. A viney, floral tattoo loops the hollow of her neck. Jackpot.

She's a succubus, known as seducers of men and hypnotic to everyone unless you can manage to tug yourself out of their powerful, exhilarating, euphoric trance . . .

I shove the sensations away like I was taught by my parents. They did a lot of training with me while I was growing up, preparing me for the day when they thought I'd become a Keeper and have to know how to protect myself from potentially dangerous, very powerful creatures.

Sucking in a breath, I peek over at Jax. Yep, he's definitely smitten by her. In fact, I think there's some drool dripping off his chin.

"I'm doing great . . . just great . . ." He dazedly grins at her then lets out a content sigh. "Just . . . great . . ."

The succubus glances me with her lips curled in delight. "You brought me a present?"

"What? Oh . . ." He blinks at me as if he forgot I was standing right next to him. "Layla, this is Alana . . . my . . ."

"Trainee." I give the succubus a cold smile. "And I'm not a present for you. Neither is Jax. So turn off the sexy charm and let him go."

She momentarily gives me a cold, hard stare, but then a massive smile spreads across her flawless face.

"Jax, she's adorable. I can see why you like her."

"He doesn't like me," I tell her, confused over her sudden personality change. "He's just stuck with me."

She laughs as if I'm being stupidly cute. "Sweetheart, trust me, he definitely likes you." She inhales then angles her head to the side. "I can smell it all over him."

I don't know what she smells, but all I get a whiff of when I breathe in is Jax's woodsy scent. And he usually smells like that.

I cough loudly into my hand to break the feelings of euphoria expanding inside me again. "So, are you going to let him out of your trance or what?"

Her lips curl as the mist from inside snakes around her. "Well, since you asked so nicely." She snaps her fingers then leaves the doorway, heading inside. "Come along and tell me why you're here. I don't have all night."

Jax gasps, blinking his eyes as he focuses on me. "What just happened?"

I point inside the doorway. "You got succubussed."

He frowns, wiping the drool off his chin. "Layla." He storms inside, disappearing into the smoky darkness. "I thought we had an agreement that you wouldn't use powers on me."

I follow after him, drawing the collar of my tank top over my nose as I make my way across an open area decorated with red velvet couches and a giant, wall-sized fish tank.

"Would you relax?" she tells him. "I was just having some fun, something you should try more often."

"I don't have time for fun," Jax says, "not with all the shit going on."

"Yeah, so I've heard," she replies through a yawn.

"You act as if this is nothing, but what's happening affects all of us."

"Yeah, yeah, yeah, chaos is threatening the world again," she says dryly. "Tell me a story I haven't heard, and then I'll react."

"What *have* you heard?" An edge carves into Jax's tone.

I track their voices to where the smoke thins and find them at a tiny bar tucked in the far back corner of the room. Layla stands behind the black marble counter, wiggling around a cocktail shaker, and Jax is perched on a stool, his rage-filled gaze on her.

"Oh, look, your adorable, little friend decided to join us." Her smile is all mocking as she sets the mixer down on the counter.

The way she keeps using the word "adorable" toward me makes me feel stupid and small, and I kind of want to kick her ass for it. But I promised Jax I'd behave, so I force my irritation down the best I can.

Jax continues to look at Layla. "Tell me what you've heard, Layla, or I won't give it to you."

Give her what, exactly?

Tons of very vivid, very succubus-like thoughts fill my mind, and I frown. The vapor clears the air as I walk up to the bar and plant my butt down on the barstool beside his. *Don't ask. Don't ask.*

"Give her what, exactly?" *Dammit! I have no self-control!*

Layla muses as she collects a martini glass from the rack hanging on the back wall. "I'm not really sure I'm supposed to tell you." Her eyes glimmer deviously as she glances at Jax. "I guess you'll have to ask Jax."

Jax shakes his head. "She's got a pretty creative mind. I'm sure she can figure it out on her own."

My lips pop open in surprise. Then disgust emerges inside me. But the emotion is erased and replaced with a more unsettling, darker sensation that burns venomously in my veins. As soon as I realize what I'm feeling, I want to bitch slap myself.

Oh, my word. I'm *jealous*. No. That can't be happening. And when the heck did this happen? I mean, the last time I checked on my girly, swoony, lovey-dovey feelings, they completely flatlined when I thought of Jax. Yeah, he's smoking hot, but he's infuriating and moody and . . .

I crinkle my nose. Is that what I like? Moody, brooding guys? I haven't had a lot of crushes before, haven't had the time.

I frown. Crap. After all that shit Jax gave me, now it turns out he was right. God, if he knew what I was thinking right now, he'd probably die from happiness.

"But, anyway." Jax coughs into his hand, attempting to clear some of the thick tension cramming the air. "Tell me what you know about what's going on."

"Jax, you know I can't tell you that kind of stuff, not when I have fey blood in my veins." She picks up the shaker and fills the martini glass to the brim with a pink liquid. "I'm bound to keep their secrets."

"There are ways around that if you really wanted to tell

me." He crosses his arms on the counter.

She props her elbows onto the counter and arches her back, her cleavage curving out of her top. "Who says I want to tell you?"

Shockingly, Jax's gaze doesn't zero in on her breasts, his eyes remaining locked on hers. "What's the price?"

She wets her lips with her tongue. "I think you know the answer to that."

"If that's the way you want to play, fine." He shoves away from the counter, standing to his feet. "Alana, wait here." He doesn't even look at me when he says it, and the jealousy switches to a stinging irritation.

"Why? Where are you going?" *Shit! I didn't mean to sound so hurt! God, would my mouth just stop opening?*

Layla evaluates me with her heavily lined eyes. "You could always come and find out."

"No, she can't." Jax winds around the counter and snags her arm. "Come on. We haven't got all night."

She grabs her martini before allowing him to whisk her across the room, passing the sofas and heading toward a dark red door on the far back wall near the fish tank.

"Such impatience." She peers over her shoulder at me, grinning impishly. "Don't worry, darling; we shouldn't be too long unless things get really, *really* good." Her lips twist into a grin. "And feel free to help yourself to whatever. Snacks. A drink." Her smile turns malicious as she takes a sip of her martini. "I think there might be some juice boxes in the fridge."

Flattening his palm against the door, he shoves his way into the room. Then he pulls her inside and slams the door without a second glance back.

I stare at the door, dumbstruck. Holy crazy land, did that just happen? And why the heck is this bothering me so much? It's not like she seduced him into going in there with her. I could tell she wasn't using her powers. He went in there under his own free will. He wanted to go.

I tap my fingers against the countertop, stewing in my confusing, conflicting emotions while obsessively staring at the door and fighting the urge to kick it down and ruin their sweaty romp in the sheets.

Eventually, I manage to regain some of my sanity and tear my attention off the door. To distract myself, I get up, wander around to the back of the bar, and search through the succubus's cabinets. I don't even know what I'm looking for other than a distraction as I open drawers then make my way into the adjacent kitchen. I browse through the cupboards then the fridge.

When I stumble across an unopened bottle of champagne, I pop the cork and drink a few swallows, partially to settle down the jealousy inside me and partly because the brand of champagne looks expensive, and I want to ruin it to get back at the succubus for calling me adorable a hundred times and telling me to drink a juice box. Beside, she's the one who said I could help myself to whatever.

I've only drunk a handful of times at the few rare parties I attended and the couple of times Jayse and I stole wine and beer out of our parents' stash. By the time I move on to snooping around her living room, my walk has a slight sway to it.

Debating where to start, my gaze skims the room and targets in on a large wooden trunk, hand carved with leafy patterns. It seems out of place with the rest of her swanky furniture and decorative wall furnishings.

"Hmmm . . . What could you be keeping in there?" Casting a quick glance over my shoulder, I tiptoe over to the trunk, flip the latch, and open the lid. My eyes widen as bright, radiating light illuminates my face. I can't see past the brightness to tell what's inside, but whatever's in there is calling to me, begging me to come to it, use the magic inside of me to find it.

"Just do it," a tiny voice says through a giggle. "You'll like it. I promise."

"Really?" I ask, knowing I should be scared, but the warmth of the glow erases the uneasiness. "What's in there?"

Another high-pitched giggle. "Come and find out. Just close your eyes and give me your hand. I'll pull you in."

I nod robotically and stick my hand inside—

"Don't touch it," a woman hisses.

Seconds later, a hand appears in my line of vision and slams the lid closed.

I jerk back, landing on my butt on the tile floor and bumping my elbow against the wall. But the pull remains inside me, pleading with me to open the trunk.

"Don't even think about it." Layla appears in front of me with her arms crossed, her mouth set in a firm line. "Do you have any idea what's in there?"

I shake my head, rubbing my tender elbow. "No."

She glances at the trunk then back at me. "Then why would you open it?"

"I don't know. I was bored." I rise to my feet. Without her heels on, I'm taller than her, and she has to angle her chin up to look at me. "And if you were worried about me going through your stuff, then you shouldn't have told me to help myself to whatever." A giggle suddenly bursts from my lips, and I slap my hand over my mouth and shake my head. "I'm sorry . . . I don't know why I just did that." I lower my hand, choking back the laughter bubbling in the back of my throat.

She purses her lips and taps her bare foot against the floor. "Jax, could you come in here? We have a situation on our hands."

"What's wrong?" Jax calls out. I hear the shuffling of light footsteps moving up behind me. "What did she do now?"

Giggles threaten to burst from my chest as I lie down on the floor and stare up at an upside down version of him. He looks too good right now, content, with his fauxhawk hair a mess and his tattooed arms hanging to his sides.

I frown, realizing why he looks so calm.

Because he just had sex . . . with Layla.

"I drank some of her champagne and opened the trunk with the giggling sprite in it," I admit through a squeaky laugh. I cover my mouth with my hand and shake my head in horror. "Jax, I think there might be something wrong with me."

"How the hell did you know it was a sprite in there?" Layla asks me with suspicion. Then her attention zones in on Jax. "What is she?"

Jax massages the back of his neck tensely. "I already told you she's a Guardian."

"Don't lie to me," she snaps, inching around me toward Jax. "If she knew there was a sprite in there, then she can hear the fey realm, which means she's at least a descendant of some fey bloodline." She gets in Jax's face and pokes him in the chest. "Why would you bring her here with everything going on? Why are you really here?" She aims a shaky finger at me. "Is she a rogue?"

He gapes at her. "A rogue? What? No, she's just a Guardian."

"Don't play dumb with me." She pokes him in the chest again, more roughly this time, and he stumbles back. "I know you have a rogue currently hiding in your school right now. You know what they are."

"Layla, I swear to God, I have no idea what you're talking about." He sounds calm, but his curled fist and stiffened stance reveal he's nervous. "I've never heard of a rogue before."

She rolls her eyes in disbelief. "Rogues are creatures who escaped those stupid experimental facilities we just talked about." She inches toward him. "They live among us, but they're not with us. They're only observing."

"Observing what?" His nervousness shifts to curiosity.

"What are they looking for?"

She shrugs. "I have no idea. Nor do I care." Her eyes narrow to slits as she zeroes in on me. "But that doesn't mean I trust them."

He blows out a gradual breath and places his hands on Layla's shoulders. "Look, Alana's not a rogue or a faerie. I can promise you that."

The muscles in her jawline spasm as she sucks in a breath through her nose and steps away from Jax, causing his hands to fall from her shoulders. "Fine, I believe you. But I want her out of here right now. The last thing I need is some strange creature trying to get into the fey realm through my entrance."

"Of course," Jax says with a nod. Then he crouches down beside me. "Let's get you out of this house so your head can clear."

"That sounds like a great idea," I agree with an exaggerated head bob. "But why's my head not clear?"

"Because you just tried to dive head first into the fey realm, and you're running on a magic high right now." He slips his arms underneath me and scoops me up. "Plus, you drank champagne for God knows what reason."

"Because I was irritated," I divulge as he carries me toward the front door.

He maneuvers the door open without putting me down. "With what?"

A cool night breeze kisses my flushed skin as we step outside, and I shiver. "Like you already don't know the answer." When he doesn't deny it, I glare at him. "Wait. Was this all part of your revenge plan? To go have gross sex with a succubus just to make me jealous?"

His boots lightly thud against the steps as he descends the stairs. "How do you know it was gross? Have you had sex with a succubus before?"

"No," I say indignantly. "But I bet it was gross . . . with her pretty eyes and her perfect body . . . Wait, what was my point again?"

He chuckles under his breath. "Before you say anything else, why don't you give yourself a few minutes to get some fresh air?"

"That's a very smart idea." I reach up and gently pat his cheek. "How come you're so smart?"

He shakes his head, fighting back a laugh. I don't know why, though. What does he think is so funny?

After five minutes of driving in the car with the window down, I start to understand.

"Oh, my God." I lower my head into my hands and slump back in the passenger seat. "I feel like the biggest idiot." I shake my head from side to side. "Why did I have to drink that champagne and open the trunk? What's wrong with me?"

"Why did you open the trunk?" Jax asks as he drives toward the center of town.

"I don't know. At first, I was just curious, but then I felt like it was . . . calling to me or something." I peek through my fingers, trying to assess him. Soft light from the lamppost lining the road outside filters into the cab and emphasizes the sheer glee in his eyes. "You're so enjoying this, aren't you?"

He wavers. "Honestly, yes and no." A small smile pulls at his lips. "I mean, it was great to hear you were jealous." His smile evaporates. "But I hate what happened with the trunk. And now Layla probably doesn't trust me." I don't know what kind of expression crosses my face, but it makes Jax react with a pleased grin. "And, for the record, I didn't sleep with her."

I eye him over, trying to tell if he's lying or not while I lie to myself, pretending it doesn't really matter.

"Then what were you doing in the bedroom for twenty minutes?"

He gives a nonchalant shrug. "Looking at that photo and

debugging your phone."

"Then why did Layla make it seem like you were going into that room to have sex?"

He fiddles with the keychain hanging from the keys in the ignition. "She was playing along with me, mostly for her own benefit. She loves stirring up trouble."

"Oh." I feel ridiculously silly, but maybe something good can come out of it. I twist the end of my braid around on my finger. "So now that we're even, can we just let this whole revenge thing go and try to be friends?"

He looks at me, sucking his bottom lip between his teeth. "Friends, huh?"

I raise my hands in front of me. "Or you can just remain the trainer, and I'll be your trainee if that's what you want."

He releases his lip from his teeth. "No, we can be friends."

"And that puts your friend quota up to what? Three?" I aim for a light joke to ease any remaining tension.

He struggles not to grin. "Actually, it's four if I include myself."

"Aw, you're friends with yourself." I press my hand to my heart. "That's so *adorable*."

Trying not to smile, he digs a stale fry out of the carton and chucks it at me. I try to do what he did earlier and catch it in my mouth, but the fry ends up nailing me in the nose.

Jax snorts a laugh. "That was attractive."

I grin. "Thanks. I tried my best."

We exchange a smile, but then any amount of humor in his eyes goes kerplunk.

"We need to talk about what I found out." He reaches into his pocket to retrieve my phone. "Whoever bugged your phone did a damn good job, and Layla couldn't trace it. But she did put an anti-charm encryption on it, so whoever was listening shouldn't be able to listen anymore."

I take the phone from him. "Good. That's one less thing I have to worry about."

"Don't get too excited yet." He pulls out onto the main road and steers the car toward the center of town. "Layla was able to translate some of the code in the painted mark."

My fingers fold tightly around the phone. "And what did it say?"

Worry overflows from his eyes as he looks at me. "It's says they'll be watching you until it's time, and then they'll come for you."

CHAPTER FIFTEEN

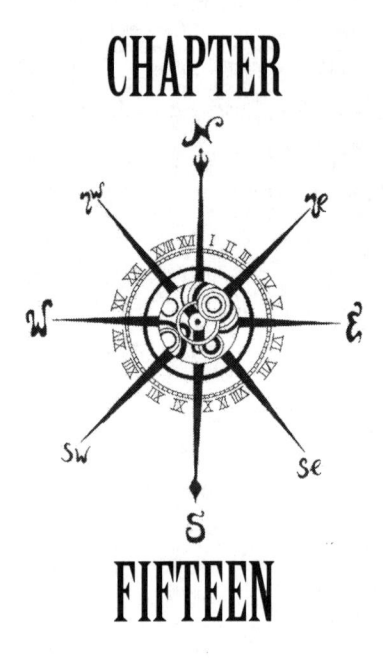

I CLUTCH THE PHONE SO tightly I nearly pop the back off. "What are they waiting for, exactly?"

"I don't know." He swallows hard. "But I think we need to keep this thing going on with you a secret for now . . . until we know for sure."

"I wasn't planning on telling anyone." I drop the phone onto my lap before I end up breaking it. "The last thing I want to do is put someone's life at risk. I probably shouldn't have even told you."

"Yes, you should've," he replies firmly. "You need to tell me everything. I can't protect you if you don't." His silver eyes smolder. "Promise me you will. Promise me that, no matter what, you'll tell me what's going on with you."

A shaky exhale fumbles from my lips. "All right," I agree.

"But only if you promise me to do the same with me."

He nods then focuses on the road. "I just wish I knew why they're sending out their experimental subjects into the real world. This whole time, I thought they were killing all of them. I mean, why kill some and let others go?"

"They're not really letting them go, though," I point out. "They're using them to watch for something, at least according to Layla. And it sounds like they brainwashed those vampires into killing the fey. Maybe that's the difference. Maybe some are useful and others aren't. Maybe some experiments are failures, and those are the ones they kill."

He looks at me with pride in his eyes. "You're getting good at this."

I shrug nonchalantly. "I guess I must have a good teacher."

He starts to smile at me, but the look vanishes as he makes a left turn into a gravel parking lot crammed with old cars and motorcycles. The area appears vacant except for a few guys loitering in front of a brick building with a neon sign that reads: *Try our special. It's to die for.* I'm sure most of the people wander in there, thinking they're going to get some amazing drink. Little do they know that they *are* the special drink.

Jax parks toward the back near a row of motorcycles, silences the engine, and takes the keys from the ignition. "I want to start here. I know a lot of vampires hang out here. Maybe we'll stumble across one from the territory clan. Or, if all else fails, we can pry some information out of one of them."

"Now you're speaking my language," I say, stuffing my phone into the pocket of my plaid jacket that is still tied around my waist.

He points a finger at me. "I want you to be careful. No doing anything irrational."

I laugh wickedly. "Ha, me? Irrational? Never."

Jax wears his infamous annoyed expression. "Alana—"

"I was just kidding," I interrupt the lecture I know he's about to give me. "I promise I'll behave and won't get into any fights."

"Don't overdo it," he says. "You can protect yourself if you need to. Just don't do anything without a cause."

I nod, reaching for the door. "That, I can do." I open the door and duck my head to get out.

Jax captures my arm. "Are you sure you want to do this? Because I can just go in."

I nod. "And for future reference, you never, ever have to double-check with me when we're about to take down the bad guys."

"You're enjoying this way too much," he says, releasing my arm.

"You have no idea." I climb out of the car, bursting with excitement as I meet him around the front of the car. "I've missed this."

"Missed what?" he asks distractedly as he checks his phone.

"Doing this kind of stuff." I gesture at the bar across the parking lot. "Going into these places and taking the bad guys down."

He puts his phone away and focuses on me. "Have you done this a lot?"

"Not as much as a Keeper." I tighten the knot on my jacket, securing it around my waist. "But I've been in my fair share of bar fights."

"Really?" he says, his voice thick with sarcasm. "That's shocking."

"I know. It's crazy," I retort, loop my arm through his, and tug him toward the entrance of the bar.

He stumbles, obviously shocked by my move, and I smile in satisfaction.

The gravel crunches under our boots as we walk side by side across the parking lot and toward the building.

When we near the door, Jax warns in a low tone, "Keep your

guard up."

The few guys hanging around outside stop talking and fix their attention on us. I don't have to see their mark to know they're vampires; I can smell the foul stench of blood oozing off them.

The taller of the three men steps in front of me as I'm about to walk through the door, moving so quickly I just about crash into him. Jax steadies me by the shoulders as I trip and nearly run into him.

Vamp dude folds his bulky arms across his broad chest, his skin strikingly pale underneath the florescent lighting of the sign. "There's a cover charge to get in."

I mentally roll my eyes, already seeing where this is heading, but I decide to play along . . . for now.

"And how much is it?"

He grins, flashing me his set of sharp, white teeth. "Well, that all depends on how good you taste." He breathes in deeply, his chest expanding. "My bet is you taste as delicious as you look." His hands shoot out, and he folds his fingers around my arm. Gripping tightly enough to leave a bruise, he jerks me toward him and dips his head to bite my neck.

I lift my knee, planning to knee him in the balls, but he suddenly gets jerked away from me. I turn around just in time to see him sail across the parking lot and collide with one of the bigger motorcycles.

Jax dusts off his hands and flashes me a cocky grin before he focuses on the other two guys who are moving in on us.

His eyes glow silver as he snarls, "So, which one of you's next?"

My heart does this stupid fluttery thing as I get a brief glimpse of his werewolf side. But even more shocking is how easily the other two vampires back down and run away, disappearing into the darkness of the parking lot.

Turning toward me, he reaches behind my back and opens the door. "Ready?"

I nod, too stunned to find my voice. I mean, holy fiery, hotness, that was hot.

He must read my turned-on expression because he lowers his lips to my ear. "I don't think that's how a *friend* is supposed to look at their *friend*."

I gently push him back, stifling a shiver. "Friends can find their friends hot when they do hot things like kick a vamp's ass." Not bothering to watch his reaction, I whirl around and march inside.

The second my feet land on the other side of the threshold, my senses are assaulted by the scent of sweat and blood. The muggy air causes my skin to dampen as I make my way deeper into the club, weaving around groups of vampires and the occasional human. While Jax chats with a vampire guy wearing leather pants and a black shirt, I keep going, searching the room for my first target.

The hypnotic beat of "Bad Blood" by Bastille begs me to join the crowded dancefloor, but I resist the desire and push my way toward the bar where three vampire guys are sitting. They look around my age, although they're probably way older, conversing and sipping from glasses filled with a thick, red liquid.

When I approach the counter lit up with neon blue lights, all of them stop talking and stare at me. Their silence and withering stares cause uneasiness to stir inside me, but I hold my chin high and approach the bartender, a taller woman with wildly brown curls and the brightest green eyes I've ever seen.

"Can I get a shot of tequila?" I plop onto the stool and nod at the vampires staring at me. "And I want to buy them a round, too."

She gives me a tolerant look. "Can I see an ID?"

I rest my elbows on the counter and give an insinuating look toward the vampires who appear around the same age as me. "You're really going to ask me that?"

She considers this before slamming four shot glasses down on the counter. "Fine." She grabs a bottle of tequila, fills the four glasses to the brim, and shoves one at me. "Drink up." Then she turns to the three vampires beside me and places a shot down in front of each of them. "She bought you a round," she says with humor in her tone.

The three of them trade an amused look, pick up the shot, and turn to me.

The one sitting closest to me flicks his shaggy, blond hair out of his hazel eyes and smiles. "I think a gesture such as this requires a toast, especially coming from such a beautiful girl."

The shorter one wets his lips with his tongue as he nods.

"I completely agree," the third says as he hops off the stool, walks over to where I'm sitting, and raises his glass. His hungry blue eyes shimmer against the dim ceiling lights. "To beautiful, violet-eyed girls."

I fake a smile and tap my glass to his. "To gorgeous guys with pretty blue eyes."

We clink glasses, and I down the shot. He sips his slowly, sucking the liquid out until he empties the glass. Then he sets the empty glass down on the counter and bites on his lip hard enough to leave indents in his lips as his eyes zone in on my neck. "I think you and I should dance." He offers me his hand, expecting me to take it.

I nod and place my hand in his, pretending to be dazzled by him, pretending I'm just a normal girl who just accidently wandered into a club chalk-full of vampires.

His icy cold fingers wrap around mine as he lifts me to my feet. Then he guides me to the center of the dancefloor beneath the shimmering lights, spins me around, and tugs me backward until my back is aligned with his chest. He starts jiving his hips, practically dry-humping me, and I pretend to be flustered, clumsily moving with him, even though I can rock sexy dance moves when I want to.

"So, how does a sweet thing like you end up in a place like this?" he asks, sweeping my hair over my shoulder.

I roll my eyes. *Cheesy much?* But it's a good line to get my plan in motion. "I was actually told by a couple of people that I should come here, that the music was great and the drinks were to die for."

"Oh, they are." His lips brush against my shoulder.

Gag me.

"I guess so. The tequila tasted pretty bitter, though," I say, rolling my hips into his.

He glides his hand down my side and molds it around my waist. "You should ask for something stronger. If you do, you might like it."

"That's what one of the people who told me to come here said," I murmur, my head bobbing backward as he slips his knee between my legs. "I bumped into her at this other club I was at a few nights ago . . . I can't remember her name, but I was hoping she'd be here because she had this cool tattoo, and I wanted to ask her where she got it. I've been wanting to get a tattoo, but it's so hard to find someone you can trust to permanently mark your body like that."

"What'd she look like?" He grazes his teeth along my shoulder, and I have to fight not to turn around and bash my knuckles against his face. "Maybe I can help you find her."

"She's a little older than us and has long, black hair. Oh, and her lips were pierced, and she has this tattoo of a red raindrop with a T at the bottom of her neck." I lean against him even though I want to pull away. "The colors were so vivid, like the ink was really good quality."

"I think I know who you're talking about. Her name's

Nadene." His teeth nick the arch over my neck, right below my pulse, as he delves underneath the hem of my shirt. "If you want, I could show you where she hangs out."

I tip my head to the side and allow him to nibble on my skin. "She doesn't hang out here?"

"She does, but she usually doesn't come in until later." His teeth are at my pulse as his hand reaches the bottom of my rib cage. "I can drive you to where she is now. My motorcycle's out back. It'll only take a few minutes."

I place my hands over his hands to stop them from moving higher. "Yeah, I don't think I want to do that."

"Yes, you do," he growls against my neck. "I can feel it."

I roll my eyes. He can't feel a damn thing, or he'd know how repulsed I am by him.

"She says she doesn't want to, so get the fuck away from her." Jax's firm, demanding voice rises over the music.

Vampire guy jerks his hands off my waist. "And who the fuck are you?"

I turn around just in time to see Jax lean into the guy's face. "The guy who's going to beat your ass if you don't get the hell away from her. Right now."

Vampire guy stares Jax down momentarily before flipping him the middle finger with both hands. "Whatever, wolf boy. But this isn't over yet." He backs away from Jax, purposely bumping his shoulder into mine.

Once he's out of sight, I smile at Jax. "That was perfect timing. Seriously, I think you might be right about us being great together."

Instead of agreeing with me, he stares at me with his arms crossed. Figuring he's pissed off at me for wandering off and tracking down information by myself, I try to smooth things over.

"I know you probably think I just broke the rules," I say as calmly as I can. "But that was me behaving. Trust me. If I was misbehaving and doing whatever I want, the conversation vamp dude and I just had would've gone down way differently." His unwavering gaze makes me squirm. "Look, I'm sorry I wandered off by myself, but I did get a name, and I do know that at least one of them will be here tonight. So, if we wait around for a bit, we might get lucky."

He continues to stare at me to the point that I feel like I'm going to burst. I'm just about to ask him what's wrong with him when he parts his lips.

"Do you always dance like that when you're supposed to be working undercover?" he asks with an inquiring look on his face.

I shake my head. Jesus, is that what this is about? What a weirdo.

"No. I usually dance way, *way* better."

"Prove it, then," he says, shocking the living daylights out of me. He doesn't seem like the dancing type.

"Um . . . what?" I look around the dancefloor then back at him as I lean in. "Is something going on that I don't know about? Are we being watched?"

"I'm just curious," he says. Then he winds around me and presses his rock solid chest against mine. When I make no move to get closer, he loops his arm around my waist and forces me closer. "Dance with me?" His diffidence makes it sound more like a question.

Figuring I was correct about us being watched, I lean against him and begin to sway my hips in rhythm. He rocks his hips with mine, his movements unsure at first, like he's trying to decide whether he wants to back out or not. I know the second he decides he's all in, though, because that's when he really starts to move.

He flattens his palms against my waist and urges me closer until our bodies are practically fused together. I rest my head back against his shoulder as he presses his cheek against the side of my head and breathes in deeply. I still don't know what's up with all the sniffing, and I make a mental note to find out. All thoughts leave my mind when his free hand also finds my waist, and he traces his fingers along the sliver of flesh peeking out of the hem of my tank top.

I uncontrollably shiver, and he chuckles, his breath dusting through my hair.

"I think you might like that a lot."

"You think so, huh?" Two can play at this game.

I reach up and play with his hair at the base of his neck, grinning when I feel a shudder ripple through his body.

"I think you might like that a lot, a lot."

He lets out a soft growl, his grip on my waist tightening as he moves his mouth toward my ear. "You drive me so damn crazy sometimes."

"The feeling's mutual." My eyelids flutter shut as he softly grazes the tip of my ear with his teeth, and I question if we're putting on a show anymore.

Another graze of his teeth. Another shudder from me . . . Or maybe it's from him. It's hard to tell with how close we are to each other. Regardless of who reacted, I find myself rolling my hips against his.

A throaty groan escapes him, his fingers digging into my flesh. I open my eyes, preparing to turn around and show him how to really dance. But mid-turn, I feel a sensation sweep over me, scorching hot and violently powerful.

The vampire who killed Adaliya is here.

I can't see her, but every one of my nerve endings magnetically connects to her. Murderous rage flames inside me, a rage I'm not sure belongs to me. But it's too overpowering to fight, and one single, all-consuming thought burst through my mind.

Find and kill her.

CHAPTER SIXTEEN

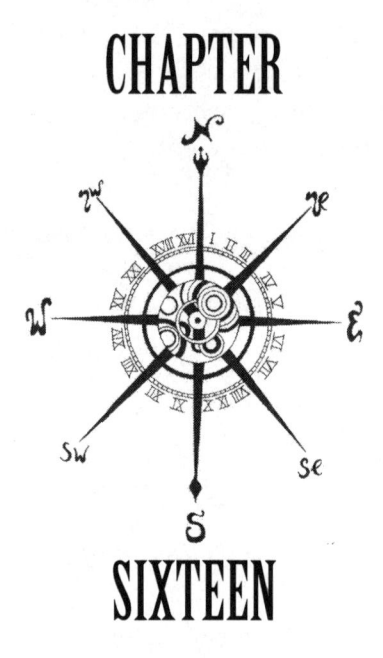

I REACT WITHOUT THINKING, MY mind no longer belonging to me . . . but to Adaliya's revenge. But as I step forward, Jax's grip on me tightens.

"Where are you going?" he whispers hotly in my ear. "We're not done yet."

I only half-hear him as I wrestle to get away from his grasp. "Let me go," I growl in a voice that sounds chillingly unlike my own.

He loosens his hold on my waist, but he doesn't release me. Then he whirls me around and looks me dead in the eyes. "What's wrong?"

"She's here . . . that vampire . . . Nadene . . ." My breaths come out and go in sharply. I'm about to start hyperventilating. I've never felt so out of control in my entire life. "I have to find her . . . kill her . . ." I look at him helplessly, begging him to understand something I don't. Maybe then he will explain to me why I feel so overpowered by the need to kill.

A pucker forms at his brow as he cups my face between his hands. I protest, wiggling to get free from him.

"Let me go," I seethe, pushing on his chest. "I need to get to her."

"No." He keeps a firm grip on my face. "I'm not going to let you go until you calm down."

"But I can't calm down," I cry, noting that some of the people around us have stopped to watch the scene unfold. I know I should stop, but I can't control the desperate need to kill the vampire I know is here.

"Yes. You. Can." His gaze never wavers from mine. "Alana, you need to realize what's happening. Remember what Ollie said about your emotions connecting to the faerie's. I think that's what's happened to you."

The light above reflects against his eyes. Music vibrates against my chest. His scent dances around me and slowly pulls me back. The longer I stare into his eyes, the calmer I feel until I manage to reclaim control over myself enough that I'm not freaking out. But I can still feel the connection to Adaliya and the desire to kill Nadene.

"Better?" he asks, and I unevenly nod. "Now tell me what's going on."

"She's here, Jax," I whisper. "She's here, and all I can think about is wanting to kill her."

He swallows hard, his fingers trembling against my face. "Tell me where she is."

"I don't know . . . I can only feel that she's here." I bite down hard on my lip as the murderous rage threatens to possess me again. "And I want nothing more than to kill her right now."

We look at each other, his worry mirroring mine, but mine

shifts into a silent plea. *Let me do Adaliya justice.*

He reluctantly removes his hands from my face and steps back. "Go find her. I'll follow."

Nodding, I eagerly turn to walk off the dancefloor and push my way through the crowd blocking the way to the door. Before I get very far, Jax snags my hand and laces his fingers through mine.

I glance over my shoulder at him and then descend my gaze to our interlaced hands. "What're you doing?"

"Making sure you don't do anything you'll regret." He squeezes my hand. "Now go."

Like a tiger tracking its prey, I determinedly move through the crowd and past the bar. The vampire I was dancing with earlier shoots me an annoyed look, but I barely register his existence, my attention focused on one thing.

Find and kill.

Find and kill.

Find and kill.

I march to the rhythm of the voice in my head, across the club and to the front door. Shoving the door open, I step outside into the chilly night air and sweep my gaze over the mostly empty parking lot until I find my target.

Her hip rests against the side of a motorcycle as she leans to the side, flirting with a human. Her back is facing me, but I know for a fact that it's her by how powerful the need to kill becomes. Potent, toxic, blinding—I can hardly think straight. If Jax didn't have a hold on my hand, I'd probably go all jungle cat on her and attack.

Thankfully, though, Jax senses my uncontrollable desire and clutches my hand securely.

"Is she out here?" he asks, stepping beside me and tracking my gaze.

I bob my head up and down. "The woman in the black dress

and heels standing over there, trying to seduced that human guy." I point at her. "That's her."

"Okay." He sticks his free hand into his pocket. "I'm going to let go of your hand. You get your ass in the car and wait for me there." He locks his dead serious eyes on me. "Under no circumstances are you to get out of the car. Got it?"

I free a trapped breath. "All right."

"I mean it, Alana." He lets go of my hand and starts to walk away, pulling a syringe out of his pocket. "Don't do anything that'll mess this case up."

I nod again and stab my fingernails into my palms until they cut through my skin. Then I focus on the pain and the blood dripping from the wounds as I head toward the car.

One . . .

Two . . .

Three . . .

I count each step as I walk, refusing to look at the vampire, knowing if I do, I'll lose my willpower. When I reach the car and duck my head to get inside, my gaze takes a mind of its own and wanders toward her just in time to see her lunge at Jax with her fangs out.

He dodges around her and swings around, moving the syringe to stab the back of her neck. But she also reels around; springs in the air, soaring at least twenty feet high; and lands on him with so much force he hits the ground like a bag of bricks. The syringe flies from his hand as she climbs on top of him and wraps her fingers around his neck. Her lips start to move. I don't know what she's saying. All I can tell is that Jax is trying to get back up, but he can't.

Just how strong is she? That thought is followed by, *What the hell did they do to her in those facilities?*

As she begins to choke him, squeezing the life from his body, my control shatters like a fragile piece of porcelain. I run to him, a scalding, unfamiliar power pulsating through my veins. I feel alive. Free. Like I could do anything. Even kill a freakishly strong vampire. And when I reach her, I let that power unleash as I barrel into her, knocking her off Jax. We slam to the ground, and the gravel tears at my skin as I wrestle to get on top of her and fasten my fingers around her windpipe. My grip tightens. My lips curl into a snarl. But Nadene only laughs, her hair sprawled around her head, her eyes sparkling elatedly. She couldn't be more relaxed.

"Stupid girl," she says. "That's not how you kill a vampire, especially not a vampire like me."

I grip more tightly until my hands ache, and she cackles, her laugh echoing across the parking lot, as she lets her head fall back. She stares up at the stars, laughing hysterically.

When her neck arches, I catch a glimpse of the tattoo on her neck. The sight of it makes my blood burn.

"Why did you kill them?" I demand. "Tell me."

"Kill who?" she says through her laughter.

I squeeze harder on her neck. "Don't play dumb. You know who I'm talking about. The North Kingdom fey."

"Oh, is that what this is about?" Her laughter dies, but the pleased smile on her face remains. "I thought this was about what's going on with you."

Icy cold fear slithers up my spine. "Why would this be about me?"

She lifts her head and whispers, "Because I know what you are."

My fingers stiffen, my heart thrashing in my chest. "You're lying."

She grins at me, her body relaxing under mine, as if she doesn't have a care in the world. "I thought you'd figured it out, but I guess you haven't gotten that far yet. I'm not lying, though. I know what you are, and I could tell you, but rogues are sworn to secrecy. If we speak of such things, we die."

I crane my fist back and bash my knuckles against her face with surprising force. "Tell me what you know! About me! About these rogues!"

She laughs maddeningly, like a person tripping on acid. "Try all you want, Alana, but you know better than to try to beat a vampire to death."

"Yeah, I do know better." I reach behind me and feel around for a sharp rock, figuring I'll bash it against her chest until it punctures her heart, but Jax crouches down in front of me.

"Let her go, Alana." His voice is steady, his gaze strong and powerful. "Let me take care of this."

My hands tremble against her neck as I shake my head. "I-I can't."

He fixes his finger under my chin, forcing me to look at him. "Yes, you can." His silver eyes glow fiercely as he carries my gaze. "You have to fight that murderous hunger you're feeling. Do you hear me? Fight. It."

It's like he completely understands the battle going on inside me, the battle to be me again and the battle to get Adaliya's revenge. My grip gradually slackens around Nadene's neck, and I lean back, winning the internal battle for the moment.

The tension in Jax's eyes alleviates as he removes his finger from my chin. "Thank God."

Nadene laughs, throwing her head back and kicking her feet as she laughs. "You're so stupid—"

Jax silences her by plunging the syringe into her neck. Her body goes limp below me as her eyelids drift shut, and her head slumps to the side.

"What was in that?" I ask as I crawl off Nadene.

"Siren's blood. Layla gave me some when we were at her place." He tosses the syringe on the ground, bends over, scoops Nadene over his shoulder, and heads toward the car. "It should knock her out for a few hours."

I follow after him, dusting the dirt and pebbles off my jeans. "Just long enough to get her back to the academy so we can question her, right?" Deep down, I know it's the right thing to do, but part of me feels severely disappointed that Nadene's blood isn't all over my hands.

He stops in his tracks and looks at me. "You did the right thing, Alana. It may not feel that way now, but after the magic in you wears off, it will. And I'm . . ." He wavers, deciding something, "proud of you."

His words soften the disappointment lingering inside of me. I cross my fingers, hoping he's right, hoping the need to kill disappears. I hope I'll be myself again.

CHAPTER SEVENTEEN

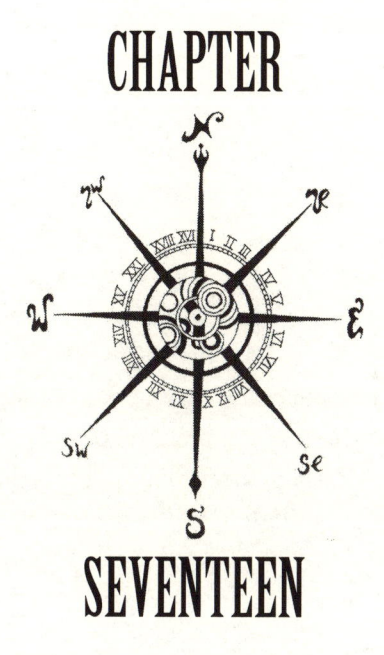

THE DRIVE BACK TO THE academy feels endless as my senses remain in tune with Nadene. Sure, Jax put her in the trunk, but the thin barrier barely puts a dent in the emotional connection I feel to Adaliya's desire to kill her.

I keep my hands balled into fists, the window rolled down, and talk Jax into letting me blast some music in an attempt to drown out my murderous thoughts. He seems in a hurry as he speeds down the highway, taking corners sharply and barely slowing down when the speed limit drops. I don't blame him. The last thing we need is to be driving when the siren's blood wears off.

We haven't talked yet about what Nadene said to me in the parking lot or what happened between Jax and me on the dancefloor. I find myself desperate to talk to him about it, to figure stuff out—well, talk about what happened in the parking lot, anyway. I'm way less eager to talk about the sexy dance moment that happened between us. That still has me super confused.

When we near the school, I lean forward in the seat and twist the volume of the radio down. "So, what comes next? I mean, what happens when we get back to the academy? Do you just put her in, like, a jail or something until she's sentenced?"

"No. First, I interrogate her and try to get a confession out of her and maybe some of the names of the other vampires who aided in the murders of the North Kingdom fey." He glances in the rearview mirror, checking on the trunk for at least the hundredth time. "But then, yes, after she confesses, she'll go to jail, wait to be tried, and then more than likely be sentenced to the Underworld where she'll endure centuries of torture by the water fey."

"Yeah, I knew about the torture part. Although, I wonder if anything will change now that they're out."

"Doubtful or we probably would've heard about it by now."

"I guess so." I stare at my hands, my fingers covered in dirt and blood. They don't feel like they belong to me anymore, but I'm certain the shame washing through me does. "She knows what I am. Nadene said she knows what I am, but she can't tell me because she's a rogue." I fold my fingers inward and elevate my gaze to him. "What if I'm something terrible? Some horrible, freakish monster who can do awful things?"

He shakes his head, rubbing at a spot of blood on his unshaven cheek. "You're not." His gaze welds with mine. "I know that for a fact."

I wrap my arm around my waist as an ill feeling twists in my gut. "How do you know that? If the Elec—*they* want me, it has to be for a reason. And considering they're murderers, I doubt that something is for the greater good."

"Just because you have powers, it doesn't mean you have to

use them for evil. Whenever a vampire or wolf is turned, they're faced with a choice: be good or be evil. Some choose the first. Others choose the latter. But it's still a choice." Keeping one hand on the wheel, he reaches over with his free hand and grazes his knuckles across my cheek. "And you'll make the first choice when and if you change."

My heart settles from the sensation of his knuckles against my skin. I don't know if he's doing some sort of freaky, relaxing wolf magic on me, but if he is, I'm glad.

"But I'm not even completely good right now," I say quietly. "I make stupid decisions. I judge certain creatures before I ever meet them."

"You may do crazy things that piss me off, but you always have a good motive for almost everything you do." He returns his hand to the steering wheel, and I internally sigh. "And as for the judgment thing, you're getting better." He brakes, slowing down the car as we near the turn off to the school. "You're a good person, Alana. I can tell."

A faint smile graces my lips. "Yeah, yeah, we'll see if you still say that tomorrow when I do something else to piss you off."

He overdramatically nods but then smiles. "You may piss me off and drive me absolutely insane, but I've never thought of you as a bad person."

"Thanks," I say. "I think, anyway."

His smile grows then fades as he parks in front of the school entrance. "Now comes the tricky part."

I unclip my seatbelt. "Why's this part tricky? Can't you just pick her up like you did in the parking lot and carry her?"

"Yeah, but I want to get her in"—he nods at the trunk—"without Vivianne knowing. If she is the princess of the North Kingdom, the last thing we need is for her to find out we have a territory vampire here." He latches onto the door handle and shoves open the door to get out.

I follow, hopping out of the car and stretching out my arms and legs. I breathe in the fresh air, my head feeling less foggy than it did minutes ago. That has to be a good sign that the magic inside me is vanishing.

After Jax shuts the car door, he rounds the back of the car and sends a text to Dash to come out and help us get Nadene inside, not because Jax can't carry her, but because he's worried she'll wake up while he's hauling her to the interrogation room.

I stand beside him, throwing glances toward the forest, questioning if anything is out there. The only light comes from the inside the school and the moonlight, and seeing farther than twenty feet away is next to impossible.

"That's strange," he mutters as he reads an incoming text. "I asked Dash about Vivianne, and he said she isn't here. She's been gone all day, and no one's heard from her."

"Maybe she's doing the same thing as us and trying to track down the territory vampires." I hug my arms around myself. "Only, she's not doing it for the case."

"I don't know." Jax's punches in something on his phone. Moments later, the screen lights up as a text pings through. He grits his teeth. "Dammit."

I inch toward him. "What's wrong?"

"Dash and his stupidity." He shakes his head. "He's been tailing Vivianne all day instead of going to his classes. Right now, he's tailed her to Glamor & Glitter & Wings, some all-exclusive fey club in New York City."

Suspicion rises inside me. "If it's only for fey, how did he get in?"

He avoids eye contact with me. "I can't answer that right now."

Well, at least he's being honest.

"I'm sure he'll be okay," I say. "And maybe it's a good thing he's tracking her. Then maybe we can find out what she's up to and if she's this princess."

"And if she's the rogue Layla told us about."

"You thought that, too?"

"Yeah, but we can't make any accusations until we find out more." He moves his fingers across buttons on his phone. "I just hope Dash is more careful than he usually is."

"I'm sure he will be," I try to assure him.

"You don't know him like I do. If you did, you wouldn't say that." He puts his phone away then turns and puts his undivided attention on me. "Thad should be out in a few seconds to help us get Nadene out to the morgue. There's an interrogation room in the basement of the school, but I'd rather this remain quiet until we hear what she says. The last thing I want is for her to blurt out more about what you are in front of a bunch of cameras and other detectives."

I glance at the forest I'm about to walk into then back at Jax. "Won't you get in trouble for doing that?"

"My supervisor might get a little irked." Noticing my wary expression, he adds, "Alana, we can't risk anyone knowing about you. It's too risky, not just for you, but for the people who find out. And with there being a rogue in the school . . ." A deafening exhale escapes his chest. "I think it's better if we keep quiet about this for now."

I'm starting to nod when Thad walks out of the school, wearing the same black jeans and dark hoodie he had on last night. He looks nervously around the grounds then trots down the steps to us. He doesn't ask any questions or seem that shocked when Jax lifts open the trunk, revealing an unconscious vampire inside.

"Where are we taking her?" Thad asks, staring into the trunk.

Jax steps up to the trunk and peers inside. "To the morgue."

Thad glances at him with confusion. "Do I even want to ask?"

Jax shakes his head. "I think the less questions you ask, the better."

Nodding, Thad reaches in, picks up Nadene, and tosses her slackened body over his large, bulky shoulder.

"I could've carried her," Jax says, slamming the trunk.

"It's okay." Thad starts for the stretch of grass that leads to the forest. "I like feeling useful."

Jax nods, stuffs his keys into his pocket, and motions for me to follow as he heads after Thad.

As the three of us reach the forest and step inside the trees, any small conversation dies between us. We walk in stiff silence, listening to owls hoot, twigs snapping, and the howling of a wolf.

"Man, I really hate this place," Thad mutters as he weaves through the trees.

"I do, too," Jax agrees, hopping over a log. "But I'm really surprised you said that, considering it seems like you and my brother were out here last night."

"We were inspecting the area for Vivianne." Thad sighs as he swings around a large rock.

"Inspecting it for what?" Jax asks, tensing when another wolf howls.

"She never said," Thad replies. "But I'm guessing she probably had us do it so she could make sure nothing was lurking around when she had that secret meeting in the forest with the empress of the Water Fey—" Thad suddenly soars through the air like a leaf blowing in the wind and lands near a thick tree with a thud. He blinks, stunned, as he staggers to his feet. "What the heck just happened?"

I open my mouth, but the words die on my tongue as I realize Nadene is no longer on Thad's shoulder.

"Um, Jax—"

He cuts me off, rushing in front of me and placing a hand over my mouth. "Shhh . . ." He tilts his head to the side, listening, but the forest is eerily quiet except for the sound of my ragged breathing.

Jax lowers his hand from my mouth and walks a circle around me. "Whatever you do, don't leave my side."

I nod, bending over and grabbing a broken tree branch from off the ground to use for a stake. Thad follows my lead and does the same before edging toward us.

When he reaches us, he rubs his shoulder and winces. "She's absurdly strong for a vamp. She's probably the strongest I've ever seen."

"Look at you. Three scared, little cowards." Nadene's shrill cackle echoes through the forest as a blur zips through the trees and zooms out in front of us.

I shuffle back as fingernails clip my cheek and draw blood. "Dammit, she cut me."

She laughs, zipping through the trees, moving so swiftly my eyes can barely track her. Leaves fly through the air, the trees begin to tremble, and birds flee from the trees.

"Think you could take me down." The blur darts back and forth in front of us, and Jax stalks the movement like prey. "You have no idea who you're messing with."

"You want to bet?" Jax starts to run forward, but an instant later, he drops to the ground, landing on his back hard.

Thad runs toward him but gets knocked down from behind and slams to the ground on his front.

Neither of them budge, and I start to fear they're dead. But the trail of moonlight sneaking through the branches above offers just the right amount of light that I can tell they're still breathing.

"You want to know why I haven't taken you down yet?" Nadene asks, her laughter hitting me from every angle.

I turn in a slow circle with the tree branch positioned to strike. "Because you're a coward."

Her laughter dies, and a roar vibrates through the ground. "How dare you insult me like that! I may be a lot of things, but I'm definitely not a coward."

"Prove it, then." My gaze sweeps the trees. "Stop messing around and come out and fight fair."

I don't expect her to take the bait, so when she appears in front of me, I startle back in shock and nearly trip over a rock. I manage to get my footing before I fall flat on my ass, though.

Regaining my balance, I stand upright with the stake raised.

Her lip twitches with delight as she stands in the center of the trees, her hair dancing in the wind. "It's like watching a child play dress up, pretending to be a warrior when really you're just a scared, little girl."

"I'm not scared." My voice comes out smooth and even. "Not even a little bit."

"You lie." Her grin challenges me. "I can smell it all over you. You're scared. Scared for yourself. Scared for your little friend over there." She glances at Jax before her emotionless eyes land back on me. "That I'll kill him, which I will. I'll kill him and the ogre, slaughter them just like my clan and I did to the North Kingdom fey." A sickeningly pleased smile possesses her face.

"You make me sick," I say, kneeing her in the belly.

She flinches, her nails piercing deep into my skin. "I'm *sick*? Just wait until you see what you can do when your powers truly come out." She leans in, putting her lips beside my ear. "Just wait until you meet the evil living inside you."

"I'm not evil." This time, my voice trembles with fear. "I could never be as evil as you."

"You think so?" She steps toward me, the leaves crunching beneath her heels. "You really have no idea what you are, do you?"

"No, but what I do know is that dress you're wearing is so unflattering on you." I use the tactic my mom taught me once as a way to throw off an opponent.

Her brows dip in confusion, and seizing the distraction, I barrel into her with the tree branch pointed at her chest. Our bodies collide, and we hit the ground hard in a tangled mess of limbs. I grapple to get on top of her, kicking her in the gut with a shocking amount of power.

She rolls to the side but flips around and comes back at me, trying to climb on top of me. Her fingers are in my hair, yanking at the roots, and her fangs glint in the moonlight.

I wiggle my arms, trying to push her off, and the tree branch clips her flesh right above her heart. Surprised I even made it that far, I feel confidence build inside me, and I move the tree branch in for the kill shot. But she snatches the branch from me and chucks it aside. Then she pins my arms down to the ground above my head, no longer laughing, but fuming mad.

"You want to know why you're going to turn out evil?" she seethes, her fingernails stabbing into my wrists. "Because you're from evil, Alana. You were raised by it."

"Liar!" I whip my head forward and knock my forehead against hers. Our skulls make a sickening cracking sound, and my head instantly begins to pulsate as the world spins around me.

Nadene barely blinks, though, gripping me as she forces my hands down into the dirt.

"You think I'm lying!" she growls, her eyes shining against the darkness. "Ask me who created me, who created all the rogues. You know him, the leader of the Electi. And really, he's your—"

Her body suddenly combusts into flames.

I scurry backward as scalding hot ash scatters through the air. I gape at the spot where the leaves and twigs sizzle with Nadene's ashes.

"What the heck just happened?"

"I think she self-destructed because she was about to tell you stuff she wasn't supposed to."

My head whips to the right and find Jax standing upright, his hair ruffled, his cheek scratched. Other than that, he looks unscathed.

Relief starts to wash through me until I realize what this means. He might have been awake and heard Nadene accuse me of knowing the leader of the Electi.

"How much did you hear?" I ask as I stumble to my feet, brushing dirt and leaves off my pants.

He plucks a few leaves from his hair, his gaze never leaving me. "All of it."

I smash my lips together, unsure what to say. While Nadene never flat-out told me who the leader was, doubt creeps into my mind that somehow it's connected to my grandpa.

Grandpa, please say something, I think. *Tell me I'm wrong.*

Silence is my only response.

"Alana, I think we need to talk," Jax starts, stepping toward me.

Then he freezes as Thad begins to stirs, his eyelids opening as he sits up and blinks. Just like that, our conversation comes to a halt, but I know this isn't over.

It's not even close.

CHAPTER EIGHTEEN

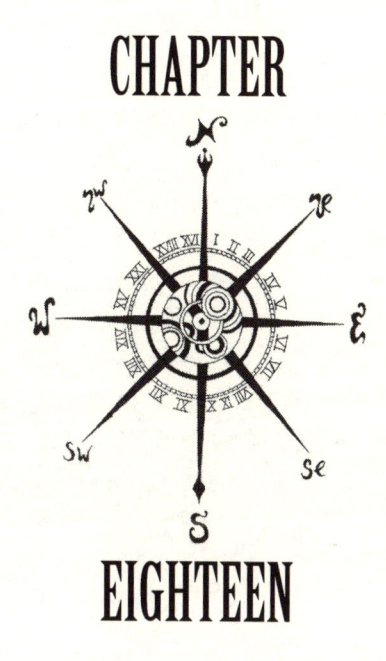

BY THE TIME JAX AND I make it back to my dorm room, the sun is starting to rise over the hills. Fortunately, the school hasn't woken up; otherwise, our appearance might set off some red flags.

Twigs and leaves stick out of my hair, dirt and grime cover my clothes, and I have bruises and cuts all over my arms. Jax doesn't look that great, either. Dark circles reside under his silver eyes, his shirt and pants are torn, and his blond hair is matted to the side.

I can barely keep my eyes open, too, and almost every part of my body aches. I want to take a shower, but the need to go to sleep is much more desirable at the moment.

"So, you're really not going to file a report on Nadene's death?" I ask, unlocking the door to my dorm room.

He shakes his head, leaning against the doorframe, watching me unlock the door. "There'd be no point. She wasn't murdered, at least not technically."

I push the door open and trudge inside the room, not the least bit surprised to see my roommate is MIA. "But what about all those fey deaths? Someone's got to pay for them."

He kicks the door shut and slips off his boots. "The territory clan will pay for what they did. My supervisor's making the arrests now."

I sink onto the bed and begin to untie my mud-caked boots. "That's good and everything, but what if none of them confess, and they go free? I'm sure the North Kingdom fey will try to kill them, but I doubt that'll happen." I grip my wrists, bruised from Nadene's grip. "Those vampires are too strong for the fey to take down."

"They don't need to confess." Jax tugs off his belt, sets it on the dresser, and walks toward my bed. "I already got a confession and turned it in."

I wiggle my feet out of my boots and scoot back on the bed. "How? We never even got to interrogate Nadene."

He stops in front of my bed. "I always record every single investigation I'm a part of." He reaches for the collar of his torn T-shirt and tugs it over his head. "I have everything on recording from the second we stepped foot into that club."

I chew on my bottom lip, trying not to stare at his ripped abs or the curving patterns of the ink tattoo up the side of his ribcage. For the briefest moment, my mind wanders back to the club when we danced together, how amazing it felt.

If only the night would've ended on that note . . .

Swallowing hard, I steady my nerves and address the problem Jax and I have been tiptoeing around since we left the woods with Thad.

"About what Nadene said . . . about me knowing the leader

of the Electi . . ." I pick at my fingernails, unable to look at him. "I'm guessing you got that on recording, too."

"Actually, I didn't." He pauses, only continuing when I look up at him. "Funny, but the recording stopped working for about thirty seconds, right about the time she said that."

I know that's not the real reason—that Jax probably did something to the recording—but . . .

"Why?" I draw my knees against my chest and recline against the headboard. "Why would you do that? You're so play-everything-by-the rules, and I'm pretty sure that's breaking a rule big time."

The mattress squeaks beneath his weight as he climbs onto the bed beside me. "I did it for a few reasons. One being I know what Vivianne will do if she heard that recording. She'll make assumptions about it being your grandfather, and then you'll get kicked out of the program." His lips pull to a lopsided smile. "And I can't lose my best partner, not when we broke the record for solving a case."

I smile at him, but the movement aches. "What're the other reasons?"

He shrugs, reaching for a pillow. "I'd rather keep those to myself."

I watch him warily as he lies down. "What about the other thing . . . ? About Nadene saying that I'm evil?"

"No one will know about that, either." He pats the spot beside him. "Now stop worrying and get some sleep. Classes start in about an hour."

I don't make a move to lie down. "You're really going to make me go to class?"

He nods, fluffing the pillow and getting situated. "The most important thing right now is for you to act normal, which means going to class. You won't be alone, though. Like I said, you'll have someone with you at all times." He pats the spot beside him again, indicating for me to lie down.

I still don't budge, eyeballing the limited space beside him and then his half-naked body.

"You're really going to sleep in my bed again? And without a shirt on?"

Amusement dances in his eyes. "You could always take your shirt off and even up the playing field."

I roll my eyes but lie down and rest my head on the pillow. Less than a minute later, Jax's eyes are shut, and his chest rises and falls with each relaxed breath he takes. I watch him sink into a deep sleep with gratitude swelling in my chest.

He may drive me nuts, but what he did for me by deleting the recording . . . Words can't even express how grateful I am.

"Thanks, Jax, for everything," I whisper softly then nuzzle deep into my pillow.

But even after the crazy night we had, my mind is too wired to go to sleep as Nadene's words replay in my mind. While I want to believe she was lying about me knowing the leader of the Electi, I can't help thinking about the cracked crystal ball tucked away in my dresser drawer, the one I'm pretty sure is my grandpa Lucas's. Jax and I found it at a crime scene where a zombie had been murdered by the Electi. I hate to think it, but I can't stop the thought from creeping into my mind. What if that's why his crystal ball was there? What if he is part of this? What if my grandpa is the leader of the Electi?

"Grandpa," I whisper. "Please answer me and tell me I'm wrong."

He doesn't answer. In fact, he hasn't uttered a word to me since Jax and I found Nadene. Whether that means something or not, I'm unsure.

I'm unsure about everything now.

All I can do is keep moving forward and try to put the pieces together before someone else does.

COMING SOON!

Enchanted (Guardian Academy, #3)

ABOUT THE AUTHOR

JESSICA SORENSEN IS A *NEW York Times* and *USA Today* bestselling author who lives in the snowy mountains of Wyoming. When she's not writing, she spends her time reading and hanging out with her family.

CONNECT WITH ME ONLINE

www.jessicasorensen.com
and on
Facebook and Twitter

OTHER BOOKS BY JESSICA SORENSEN:

Broken City Series:
Nameless
Forsaken
Oblivion (coming soon)

Entranced Series:
Entranced
Entangled
Enchanted (coming soon)

Rebels & Misfits Series:
Confessions of a Kleptomaniac

Honeyton Series:
The Illusion of Annabella

Sunnyvale Series:
The Year I Became Isabella Anders
The Year of Falling in Love
The Year of Second Chances (coming soon)

The Coincidence Series:
The Coincidence of Callie and Kayden
The Redemption of Callie and Kayden
The Destiny of Violet and Luke
The Probability of Violet and Luke
The Certainty of Violet and Luke

The Resolution of Callie and Kayden
Seth & Greyson

The Secret Series:
The Prelude of Ella and Micha
The Secret of Ella and Micha
The Forever of Ella and Micha
The Temptation of Lila and Ethan
The Ever After of Ella and Micha
Lila and Ethan: Forever and Always
Ella and Micha: Infinitely and Always

The Shattered Promises Series:
Shattered Promises
Fractured Souls
Unbroken
Broken Visions
Scattered Ashes

Breaking Nova Series:
Breaking Nova
Saving Quinton
Delilah: The Making of Red
Nova and Quinton: No Regrets
Tristan: Finding Hope
Wreck Me
Ruin Me

The Fallen Star Series (YA):
The Fallen Star
The Underworld
The Vision
The Promise

The Fallen Souls Series (spin-off from The Fallen Star):
The Lost Soul
The Evanescence

The Darkness Falls Series:
Darkness Falls
Darkness Breaks
Darkness Fades

The Death Collectors Series (NA and YA):
Ember X and Ember
Cinder X and Cinder
Spark X and Cinder

Unbeautiful Series:
Unbeautiful
Untamed

Made in the USA
Middletown, DE
19 June 2016